I0557205

DEEP
IN THE
SHALLOWS

A Lake Waihola Mystery

J. L. O'Rourke

Millwheel Press Ltd

Published by:
Millwheel Press Ltd
Eyrewell Forest, New Zealand
www.millwheelpress.co.nz

ISBN 978-0-473-41592-1 – Softcover
ISBN 978-0-473-41593-8 – epub
ISBN 978-0-473-41594-5 - mobi

Acknowledgements

Thanks to John and Lucy whose old house I have twisted into the Netherby house and who were the owners of the real Kali pug whose swimming antics gave me the original idea for the plot, and to Joanne Nicolson, owner of the real Jackson whippet.

Thank you to Swanndri, the clothing company, for allowing me to use their company name and their iconic brand of jackets to clothe my Southern Men.

All the characters in this book are fictitious. No relationship is intended to anyone living or dead. The Waihola buildings and campground are real but the people I have put in them are entirely fictitious.

The Netherby house does not, in actuality, border the lake – the house I based it on is several kilometres away up a back-country road. I have taken substantial liberties with its condition and layout.

Andrea North sees a job at beautiful Lake Waihola as a welcome escape from her controlling ex, but an easy task is soon complicated by a strange hoard and a close encounter with an arrogant pig hunter. When the campground dog pulls a gruesome object from the lake, Andy must decide who is she fighting against and who she can trust.

Chapter 1

I was sure I was going backwards. Actually, I wasn't. The plane was still moving forwards, descending rapidly towards the land, but it felt more like a time machine travelling back into my past than a small jet in a standard landing manoeuvre against what I knew would be a strong crosswind. I pulled my seatbelt tighter, sat back and braced myself. There was always a crosswind at Momona airport but that wasn't the reason I was wriggling in my seat, nerves on edge. Did I really want to be here? Was this journey a blessing or a curse?

As if in answer the small plane rocked, buffeted sideways as the wind hit it. Around me, gasps of fright and clenched knuckles distinguished the first-time visitors from the local travellers. I stifled a giggle as I recognised in them the fear I had felt, and conquered, years ago, while the captain's cheerful words from the intercom welcomed us all to Dunedin.

"I hope all you North Islanders brought a raincoat," he added. "It's a bracing nine degrees out there this morning, with a gusty south-easterly, although they tell me that the rain should ease by this afternoon. Thank you for flying Southern Air."

In a series of sways and bumps, the plane touched down, rumbling to a halt in front of the white rectangle that was the terminal building. With my fellow weary travellers I stumbled down the metal steps, pulling my casually comfortable clothes tight against the weather as I scurried across the rain-soaked tarmac to the protection offered behind the welcoming entrance door. Safely inside, I shook the rain from my jacket, looked around and sighed in despair. Nothing had changed since I had last made the same journey. I had hoped to see some changes, not the same old walls with the same old memories. It didn't bode well. Was this going to be a new start or a dreadful repeat of past mistakes? At least the terminal was warm.

With no desire to go back out into the rain and worry about what I was heading towards, I did what I always do when there's a decision to be made. I procrastinated. Trailing behind the other travellers, I let them forge ahead to claim their baggage, content to let my own bag circle past three times before I stepped forwards to wrestle it from the carousel. I wasted more time amusing myself watching an anxious tour guide goad and cajole into order his flock of recalcitrant human sheep, their excited exclamations of wonder overpowering his futile instructions to board the bus parked outside the terminal's main door. I checked my watch. A bit early for lunch but I could smell coffee. Waihola would wait for me; another hour wouldn't make any difference. Dragging behind me my garishly striped suitcase with the faulty wheel, I clattered my way across to the café, ordered a large long black and a blueberry muffin, struggled to balance the tray in one hand and steer the suitcase with the other, then gave up, dividing the tasks into two journeys to the closest table and chair, into which I collapsed with a profound sigh of relief and an admission that I would never make a successful career as a waitress.

Not that I needed a career as a waitress, I had a much better one, even if I was bored with the corporate clothes, the tiny air-conditioned office with its neat desk and ordered filing system, the repetitive sameness of every day. It had a fancy title though. Executor of wills and estates for Wilson Smythe, an important firm with connections to all the right people and branches in several cities. I worked with dead people. Or to be precise, I sorted their estates after they died and made sure all the conditions of their wills were carried out. Which is why I was heading to Waihola. I wasn't sure if the boss had sent me because I used to be a local, so I was less likely to get lost than my city-slicker workmates, or because she knew what was going on in my private life and was being kind, giving me a week out of town to help get the message through to Simon. Either way, while part of me was feeling strange about returning to Otago, more of me was pleased to be getting out of Wellington.

The big choice was whether I actually wanted to go back there. Did I want to go back to the city after I had finished this job or did I want to stay as far away as possible? My workmates had been supportive and encouraging but he had demanded. He had assumed that I would do as he said. He was wrong. I had been astounded at his assumption that I would do as he ordered and infuriated by the continuous string of angry texts and emails he had sent since I had defied him to do my job. That thought made me remember my mobile phone. I rummaged in my jacket pocket, drew it out and reset it from flight mode. The texts pinged as they arrived. Twenty. In the time it had taken to fly from Wellington to Dunedin, he had sent twenty texts. I deleted them all unread. At least I was in the other island. There was no more danger of him barging into my flat or parking his car in the street outside for hours, watching me.

I leant back in the chair, the taste of freedom blending with the blueberry muffin and the smell of coffee. My phone pinged again. Another text from him. Shaking my head in disbelief, I thumbed the contact icon and clicked on his details. A few keystrokes changed Simon Briggs to Simon Bastard. Then I deleted his text, still unread. There were several emails as well. I deleted all the ones from him and scanned the others, leaving them unopened to deal with later. Nothing required my urgent attention. There wasn't going to be anything that required my urgent attention this week. Certainly nothing in Wellington. I checked the time. Time to move. I had to do it sometime, I couldn't set up camp in the airport. Remembering all the tips from the corporate empowerment workshops he had dragged me to, I downed the last of the coffee, stood, squared my shoulders and marched towards the rental car facility, dragging my reluctant luggage, squealing in rebuke, behind me.

Behind the counter, the rental car agent's cherry-lipsticked smile failed to reach her bored eyes as she proffered the standard greeting.

"I have a car booked," I smiled back in a friendly gesture that made no difference.

"Name?"

"North. Andrea North."

"Driver's licence?"

Still smiling, I opened my wallet, flashing my licence in its plastic sleeve. The bored woman gave it a cursory glance before pushing her paperwork forwards for my signature and handing me a set of keys.

"It's parked out there," the agent drawled, pointing to a door to her left. "It's the grey Mitsubishi hatchback. The registration number is on your keys."

Dismissed, I forced my reluctant luggage in the direction indicated, pushing through the door to find that the car was where it was supposed to be and the rain had cleared. Next stop, Lake Waihola where my oldest memories would become my new life – at least for a week.

Once in the car though, I had an overwhelming desire to drive the other way. It was tempting to take the road north to Dunedin where I could hide away in the old buildings of the university campus, instead of turning south towards the lake and the task I had been given.

"Get a grip!" I scolded myself. "Breathe in. Treat this as a holiday. A deceased estate near the lake. All you have to do is sort the old lady's stuff, value it, organise someone to pack it up, then hand the house over to a real estate agent to sell. How hard can that be? And stop talking to yourself or people will think you're crazy."

There was only a flash of indecision when I reached the crossroads. One quick glance in the direction of Dunedin, a deep breath, and I turned the car south. I turned up the radio, singing along to an old country song as I crossed the Taieri Plains. I had always loved the secret way the lake suddenly appeared as the car swept around the bend in the road. I would crane forwards in the back seat of Dad's car, trying to be the first to shout, "I see the lake!". Driving my own car around the bend was just as magical. I revelled in the first sight of the blue water, letting pleasant memories of childhood lakeside picnics outweigh the nagging doubt that I was heading towards something momentous that would force me to make decisions. I hated making decisions.

But where had that got me? An inability to make decisions

had led to me leaving the decisions to others, then blindly following whatever they suggested, even if it wasn't what I had wanted to do. In the end, it had led to working in a job I was bored with, because that was easier than pushing myself to do something new, and going out with a man who treated me like his personal slave. No more! When I had packed my bag to fly south, I packed only my pyjamas, an old pair of jeans, a spare t-shirt, a woollen jersey Mum had knitted for me several years ago and one uncrushable, bland business suit, just in case. All the exquisite designer dresses that he had bought and ordered me to wear were left behind, in a rubbish bag dumped outside my neighbour's door with a note asking her to donate the bag to the Salvation Army. I was wearing my better pair of jeans, my favourite t-shirt and a comfortable grey jersey under my waterproof hooded jacket. When I needed more, I would treat myself to a shopping spree in Dunedin – even if that would mean making my own decisions.

I slowed down as I drove into the tiny township of Waihola. It had hardly changed since I had last visited – how many years ago? I could see some new houses on the sloping hill to my left, but the Black Swan Café was still there. In the centre of the town I turned right, towards the lake, and pulled into the campground, stopping in front of the small office. As I stepped out of the car a smiling woman in overalls and gumboots waved from the nearby ablution block. She hurried towards me, almost tripping over a rotund black pug that weaved around her legs as she approached.

"Hi," she greeted, "I'm Gail. My husband, Tom, and I run this place. You must be Miss North."

"Yes, Andrea North. I've got a cabin booked but I'm not sure how long I'll need it for."

"That's not a problem, dear. It's not the busy season yet, so there's not exactly a horde of campers waiting in line. You just let me know from day to day and we will sort it all out. Now, come inside and we'll do the paperwork."

Ten minutes later, I placed my suitcase on the metal-framed bed that took up most of my tiny cabin, turned, and gazed out the door to the clear, blue waters of the lake, stretching across the landscape from its beach, just a few metres away. I tasted the scent of the recent rain on the crisp, fresh air. As I breathed in, my mobile phone pinged. Another text message from him. This time I didn't delete it, but opened it and typed a reply.

What part of NO do you not understand! F off!!!

Muttering a curse, I hit send, thrust the phone into my pocket and strode off towards the lake. That felt good.

My attitude surprised me. A month ago, even a week ago, I wouldn't have dared speak back to him, and I certainly wouldn't have used the F word. I would have hung my head, avoided eye contact, apologised even if I had done nothing, and sat meekly while he lectured me about my myriad of faults. The memory of how low I had fallen refuelled my anger, spurring me towards the soothing pull of the lake, away from the cabin, away from reality. If I had been in Wellington city work mode, I would have stayed in the cabin, dragged the paperwork out of the side pocket of my suitcase, searched the internet for the address then headed out to look at the house I was supposed to be evaluating, but the lake was so peaceful that work seemed like a lifetime away and Simon seemed like another universe, one that was now well behind me.

How had I allowed myself to become so pathetically dependent? It had taken two years, even with the warnings from my friends, to realise how controlling he was, then another five months to pluck up the courage to leave, but one text from him was still enough to rocket my anxiety levels. I purposefully slowed my pace, breathing out the anger that welled at the mere thought of him, relishing the joy that came with feeling my own new strength. Blowing Simon out, breathing the lake in, I allowed myself to meander along the gravel footpath that stretched beside the edge of the lake, inviting me to follow it to its end. The quiet was almost overwhelming. My memories of Waihola were from school holidays and summer weekends when the campground was full of tents and caravans with mothers still carrying out the basic day to day chores of cooking and cleaning, but out of plastic buckets, yet still smiling while their rambunctious children, myself included, ran riot, throwing themselves into the weedy water heedless of their parents warnings to look out for hidden dangers. I had always thought Waihola was too peaceful to hide any danger.

Shrugging off the work-ethic induced voice that nagged at the corner of my brain, reminding me of the paperwork and the house I was supposed to be finding, I continued my slow walk until the path came to its end at a solitary wooden picnic table on a small promontory. I was tempted to sit for a while and gaze at the lake, thinking nothing, but it was obvious that the ducks had been there before me. Even though they weren't my best clothes, I wasn't willing to risk the one tiny clean patch available on the wooden seat, so I was left with the only sensible alternative. I turned around and made my way back to my cabin, wondering if, somehow, the ducks and my guilty conscience were working together. At least I had discarded the thoughts of Simon; the deep lake a much better antidote than Wellington city had been.

Back in my cabin I forced myself to concentrate on the job I was supposed to be doing. A glance at my watch proved that I still had at least three hours of daylight, which was more than enough time to find the house, even if the real work waited until tomorrow. The information I needed was all in the fat legal file that I pulled from my suitcase. Ignoring the will and the other estate documents, I spread out the topographical map and the handy internet-sourced aerial photograph. Both had the property conveniently marked with a large X in red felt pen, but even without that I knew I could find the place easily. When we were children, while we played in the lake and Mum lounged on a deck chair reading romance novels, Dad would sneak off to the pub where he made friends with the local farmers, shouting them beers and beating them at darts. On rainy days, when the lake wasn't an option and the caravan was too crowded, Dad would bundle us into the car and drive to one of their farms where we would traipse through muddy paddocks in shorts and gumboots while Mum talked about us and Dad drank more beer. So, as I looked at the map, I was reasonably certain I knew where I was going.

The property was a small holding just to the south of the lake. I took careful note of the road names, grabbed my keys and set out, counting side roads as I drove even though I had programmed the GPS. A right turn off the highway, another right then a left and I was off the tarmac onto gravel. I hadn't accounted for that. Or, rather, I had expected the roads to be gravel but I hadn't realised my city driving skills would be so inadequate. My memories were of Dad effortlessly throwing the family Valiant around the bends, gravel spraying from the bite of the tyres on the verge – my reality was sudden panic as the lightweight rental began to slide. Just before I did something stupid and hit the brakes, one piece of Dad's advice popped into my head. Don't brake! Heart pumping, hands rigid on the steering wheel, I took my foot off the accelerator and, as the car slowed down, concentrated on keeping it going in a straight line down the middle of the road. Back in control, I breathed again then continued up the road at a much slower speed, heart pounding, lesson learnt.

I soon realised my childhood memories were faulty - a couple of twists in the road and I had lost all sense of direction. Ahead I could see an intersection, maybe even a signpost, so I risked stealing a sideways glance at the map that was spread out on the passenger's seat. The red X was off to the right, just where the GPS kept telling me it would be. Confident that I wasn't lost, and feeling better about my country-road driving skills, I sped up a little, imagining myself rally-driving around the corner, channelling Dad and the Valiant as I turned the steering wheel.

I avoided the head-on collision.

A mud-encrusted Land Rover rushed towards me, using more than its share of the road, forcing me to take evasive action. In a split second I whipped the wheel to the left, slammed on the brakes and hung on as the car spun in a giddy circle before coming to an abrupt halt in the roadside ditch, back wheels in a hole, front facing back the way I had come. The dead pig on the Land Rover's tray bounced as it disappeared around the bend.

"Bastard! Arsehole!" There was no point yelling, neither the driver nor the pig could hear me, but it released the tension and was a better alternative than bursting into tears, which were threatening as I realised I might be stuck in the ditch. Breathe! I turned the key, sent up an amorphous prayer to the roadside fairies, and tried the accelerator. The fairies were kind. With a shuddering lurch the car pulled itself out of the ditch, although in my surprise I almost forgot to stop accelerating and nearly ended up in the matching ditch on the opposite bank. With my imagination conjuring images of more vehicles ploughing into the side of me while I was broadside across the road, I spun the wheel to straighten the car, faced it in the right direction, threw a few more choice expletives back in the direction of the vanished Land Rover, then continued my journey up the hill, hugging the left hand side of the road and vowing never to accept jobs up country roads again.

I had only travelled a few hundred metres, and my heart rate hadn't yet returned to normal, before the GPS told me I had reached my destination. The name on the open five-bar gate confirmed it. I pulled the car onto the unkempt grass driveway, following its track down the side of the house to a dirt parking bay in front of a raised wrap-around deck.

"Wow!" I really should stop talking to myself. Not "wow" spectacular, amazing, fabulous. More "wow" unique, crazy, am-I-really-seeing-this. From the front the house looked like a picture-book farmhouse with large, white-painted French doors opening onto the deck from several rooms, all with panoramic views over the paddocks down to the lake, but the view as I had driven in had already shown the house's odd secret – it was two houses joined together on a crazy angle, an ungainly marriage of a villa and a cottage. A work in progress, incomplete.

I left the car, locked it automatically as you do when you live in the city, then walked back down the drive. Before I let myself into the house I had to see it from all sides. I wasn't disappointed. Every side was different. It was soon obvious that the cottage had been in poorer condition than the villa when they were moved there and stuck together. The back of the house, the cottage part, showed sheets of plywood tacked over rotting weatherboards, disintegrating window frames and a large tarpaulin nailed over what must have once been a back door. Then, as I made it all the way around to the villa, the house was a different creature with aluminium windows, a reasonably recent paint job and a surprisingly healthy garden of succulents and cacti thriving under the stairs to the deck.

I checked my watch. It was tempting to go inside and look around but I could wait until tomorrow. My objective had been to find the place and I had done that. Now I was hungry, so a better plan was to drive back to Waihola to find somewhere that served my idea of fine dining – fish and chips. The Bastard would not have approved.

The drive back to the camp was delightfully uneventful – no hurtling dead pigs chauffeured by idiots – but I was relieved to pull into the carpark beside my little cabin. Still in city mode, I locked the car, leaving the map but grabbing my jacket. The wind was picking up as the temperature dropped, creating choppy waves with tiny white tops across the blue expanse of the lake. I heard two swans shrieking complaints against the rising tide. Above the water dark clouds threatened another downfall of rain. If I was going to get food I needed to do it soon, while I was still warm and dry. I pulled on my jacket, zipping it all the way to the neck as I walked, head down against the rising southerly wind, back towards the main road where I knew there were the essentials of every small town – a dairy, a pub, a garage, and a fish and chip shop.

My first stop was the dairy. I would need something for breakfast tomorrow, and something to take with me up to the house as I expected to be there all day and didn't fancy driving back for lunch. Then, clutching my purchases of coffee, bread, milk, jam, margarine and a packet of the chocolate biscuits that I loved but Simon disapproved of, I carried on past the pub to complete my mission. That's where I saw the Land Rover, pig still lolling on the tray, parked in the pub carpark. I wasn't surprised. It seemed perfectly logical that any man who killed pigs and drove like a maniac would end his hard-working day at the local pub. I was tempted to go in and tell him what I thought of him and his driving, then I realised I was tempted and was startled at my burst of courage. Where had that come from? A few weeks ago I wouldn't have dared have a determined thought like that. I shook my head in disbelief at my own energy, then giggled to myself as I realised how silly I would look, confronting the whole bar when I had no idea who the man was.

I carried on to the fish and chip shop to buy my order which I ate, like a naughty child, ripping a hole in the end of the newspaper wrapping as I wandered back to my cabin. Kali the black pug, named after the fearful Hindu goddess to whom she bore no resemblance at all, apart the permanently protruding tongue, met me halfway, her fat body making ridiculous attempts at jumping that her short legs couldn't sustain, her tongue and ears flapping out of time with her leaps. I fell for the routine and handed her a chip that barely touched the sides as she snorted it down. I was going to give her another one when Gail's voice stopped me.

"Don't let her con you into feeding her – she's supposed to be on a diet."

"Sorry."

"She's naughty," Gail caught up with me and gave Kali a pat on the top of her head. "The vet has told us that she has to lose weight, but she's pretty good at doing that pathetic starving look, even though she's the size of a bus. And if she can't scavenge food off us, she knows the campers will feed her." She turned to the dog. "You're a very bad dog!"

Kali, rightfully, took the pleasant tone of voice as praise rather than reprimand and panted her enjoyment at the attention. I laughed and gave her a pat.

"Next time, pooch, when no-one's looking."

"Are you settled in okay?" Gail asked.

"Yes, no problems," I replied. "I've found the place I have to value and I will get started tomorrow. Hopefully it won't take too long."

"That's Maggie Netherby's place, isn't it? Have they figured out what to do with it now?"

"Yes and no. Yes it is Margaret Netherby's house that I am here to value, but no, there are still some complications with the will and the inheritance before it can go to probate and be settled."

"Let me guess, there could still be some relatives somewhere waiting to pop out of the woodwork and claim the farm?"

"Something like that," I laughed. "But that's not my department. I just have to make an inventory of her stuff. Boring paper work, that's my specialty."

"Well, if you're sorting her stuff you are going to be busy." She smiled at my confused expression. "Maggie was a hoarder. You might need to organise a rubbish skip."

"Oh, great."

With those inspiring words of comfort, Gail rounded up Kali and left me to continue to my cabin, munching thoughtfully on a tender piece of cod, or shark. A hoarder. Someone could have warned me. Oh well. As long as she didn't hoard dead pigs.

I dumped my meagre groceries onto my bed, plonked myself on the other end and spread my fish and chip wrapping out beside me so I could finish my meal, while trying not to think about how much extra work this job might now entail. I needed coffee. I fished my favourite travel mug from my luggage and ventured out into the now chilly air to find the communal kitchen and some hot water.

The camp's kitchen was a large, well-appointed hive of activity. To reach it I had passed a cluster of tiny one-man tents beside a dusty mini-van, so I wasn't too surprised to find the kitchen full of fit young German tourists, all talking at the top of their voices. One of the girls gave me a hard stare as I slid past them to the other end of the bench where I could see a lone electric jug. I filled it rapidly without looking at my fellow campers. It wasn't that their presence irritated me, I just couldn't be bothered making small talk, let alone translating it, so I avoided eye contact while the jug boiled then filled my travel mug and hurried back out into the fading light. As I didn't feel like sitting in the tiny cabin, or chatting with the Germans, I figured my best option was to walk aimlessly around the camp, sipping coffee as I ambled.

I didn't consciously head towards the lights, it just seemed like the natural thing to do. Without any logical thought or plan, I found myself wandering along the edge of the railway line that separated the campground from the shops on the main road. Through the trees I could hear, although I couldn't see, the business machinations normally hidden from the customers. Behind the fish and chip shop I heard a growled, "Get out of it, you manky shit," followed by something being thrown and a cat screech in complaint as the object found its target. From further along I could hear the dairy owner stacking crates, grunting as each one thumped into its allotted place. The interesting stuff was between the two. A man's voice, with a real Kiwi "Southern Man" accent, just like the old guy on the beer advertisements, carried easily on the wind.

"Nice one, mate. She's a big bitch all right. You'll get a few pork pies out of that one, Bill."

"Yep," a second voice agreed. "Reckon I will."

"Bring her down to the shed, mate, and we'll get her hung up. I'll cut her up tomorrow."

A third, younger voice, joined in. "Okay. Tom, you go and open up and I'll follow you down. Hey Bill, you'd better save me some of those pies."

Tom. With a speedy deduction worthy of Sherlock Holmes, I realised that one of those voices had to belong to Gail's husband. She'd said his name was Tom. So Bill had to be someone who made pies and the other voice must have been the driver of the Land Rover, as my super deductive powers worked out that the dead pig must be the potential pie source. All of a sudden I was angry again at his bad driving and I wanted to know why he hadn't stopped to see if I was hurt. Swallowing the last of my coffee, I aimed for the office and manager's house, where I figured the pig butchers were heading.

I came around the side of the house just as the Land Rover pulled in, turning to back into a huge shed almost as big as the house. The man I assumed was Tom was standing beside the opened roller door, waving directions to the driver as he reversed. I waited until he had turned off the ignition and stepped out of the vehicle before I marched up and gave him both barrels.

"Hey, you!" I stepped in front of him so he had to know I was aiming my anger at him. "Yes, you! Do you always drive like a dick?"

He looked confused. He also, as I drew back a pace to draw breath, looked gorgeous, but I was too angry to let a little thing like light-brown hair with blond streaks flopping over blue eyes set in a tanned and perfectly angled face, put me off my stride. He continued to mime confusion, spreading his hands, palms up, and making noiseless movements with his mouth.

"A couple of hours ago," I reminded him. "Country road, south of the lake, blind corner, some idiot, who I may or may not be talking to right now but drove a Land Rover with a dead pig on the back, cut me off and forced me into a ditch, then sped off into the dust. I could be still stuck there, in that bloody ditch, for all you knew or cared. I could be bloody dead in the bloody ditch!" I stopped before my voice reached screeching pitch. I was shaking again.

Mr Too-Gorgeous-To-Be-True raised a hand to cover his open mouth in a gesture I had to admit looked genuinely like shock.

"You're right. I drive like a dick. It's a bad excuse but I am so used to having that road to myself."

"Yeah, it's a bloody awful excuse. And it doesn't explain why you didn't stop to make sure I was all right!"

"I knew you were all right. It's not that big a ditch. And I was in a hurry, it was an emergency."

"An emergency? Yeah, I could tell that by the fact that you were parked at the pub by the time I got back. Can't let a cold beer get in the way of road safety, can we?"

Before he could answer I turned on my heel and stormed off. By the time I had reached my cabin I had run out of colourful swear words and my anger had diffused enough to let in other thoughts. Like how much I needed another coffee. This time the communal kitchen was empty, a small fact for which I was grateful as I boiled the jug and refilled my travel mug. All of a sudden my cabin seemed like a nice place to be.

Until the gun shots woke me up.

Chapter 2

After the coffee and the rant at the good-looking idiot, it took me a while to calm down. I forced myself to stop thinking about how his eyes sparkled and concentrated on reading through the paperwork on the Netherby estate, which was a good tactic as there is nothing more soporific than comfy pyjamas, a warm bed and a boring legal document. Eventually I drifted off to sleep to the gentle lullaby of birdlife and lapping water. I was riding a pig up a country road somewhere in dreamland when the pig was shot out from underneath me. One minute I was on the pig, moving fast, then I was on the ground, flat on my back, watching the pig roll away. It waved its trotters in the air, snorted, then turned into a Land Rover, out of which stepped a handsome man, no, a handsome pig with blond-streaked hair. He stretched out a trotter to help me up but his arm became a gun. Bang! He shot me and I woke up.

A third shot. I looked at my watch. Twenty minutes after midnight. What sort of a place was this? I hugged my knees, wrapping the blanket tight around me, waiting for the sound of police sirens which I was sure would quickly follow the sound of gunfire. Nothing happened. No sirens, just the occasional rumble of a truck along the road. An overwhelming need for air made me realise I had been holding my breath. I gulped, breathed and loosened the tight hold on my knees and the blanket, easing the muscles that had begun to shake with the tension of holding myself together. Still expecting police sirens, I crept out of bed, wrapped my blanket around my shoulders for comfort more than for its warmth, and peered out the cabin's tiny window. Nothing. The camp ground was quiet. Gradually I convinced myself that I had been mistaken. It could have been any kind of country noise. It might not have been a gun. I wriggled back into my bed and drifted back to sleep.

One of the benefits of being an island away from him was not being on "Simon time", so I didn't feel at all guilty when I finally woke up a good hour and a half after the usual Wellington morning panic. I didn't feel pressured to rush up to the Netherby house, so I took my time. Once again the communal kitchen was full of excited Germans, but this time I joined in, listening to, if barely understanding, their plans for the day and correcting their pronunciation of the local place names. Then I took my toast and coffee and wandered down to the lake to watch the swans. There were a lot more of them than I remembered. Between my childhood holiday visits and my return, the swampy wetlands at the northern end of the lake had become a protected reserve, so wildlife of all kinds had flourished. I wandered along the lakeshore, fascinated by the little scaups, even reverting to the silly game I used to play when I would watch a scaup dive then try and hold my breath till it popped up again. I have never succeeded. Further out from the shore several pairs of black swans floated with serene elegance in complete contrast to the effervescent bobbing scaups.

As I sauntered past a dilapidated jetty, a scaup shot out of the water at high speed, its sudden appearance making me spill my coffee. I peered at the water to see what had frightened the bird, then laughed out loud as the culprit surfaced. With only a nose bobbing out of the water to snatch breaths, her body fully submerged, Kali the fat pug swam out from under the jetty. I called her name, then laughed again as she struggled out of the water, determinedly dragging a tree branch, complete with sodden leaves.

"You silly dog," I praised her, patting her head while avoiding her attempts to shake herself dry. "Does your mother know you're trying to drown yourself?"

"She does it all the time," a voice behind me answered. I turned to find Tom striding across the grass. "She don't look like much of a water dog but we can't keep her out of it."

"She looked so funny swimming – I could only see her nose poking out."

"Yeah, beats me why she doesn't sink like a stone. Anyway, lass, I saw you down here and thought I should check up and see if everything's okay. You sounded real pissed off with Brownie yesterday, so I thought I should ask."

"Brownie? Is that his name? The guy with the dead pig?"

"Yeah, that's him. He's a good guy, really."

"Okay – he's a good guy who drives like he owns the road."

Tom laughed. "You get used to that around here. Country roads, bugger-all traffic. I guess we should all be a bit more careful."

"Yes! Yes you should. He should, anyway."

Tom looked suitably abashed as he turned to leave, patting his thigh for Kali to follow. I put my hand out, touching his jacket to regain his attention.

"Tom?" He turned back to face me. "Tom, did you hear those gunshots last night?"

"Gunshots?"

"Yes, three of them, I think. About midnight."

Tom shook his head, shrugged his shoulders and flapped his hands at the same time in a movement that showed complete bafflement.

"Nah, sorry, didn't hear a thing. I suppose it could've been rat shooters, up at the dump."

"Rat shooters?"

"Yeah, there's a big problem with rats at the dump. They breed in the rubbish. Shooting them's a popular sport with the young folk. Not much else to do and it keeps their eye in for pig shooting. It was probably just some young blokes. The dump's just up the hill there," he waved his arm vaguely in the direction of the road, "so the sound probably travelled if the wind was right. We wouldn't notice, we're used to it. If we don't notice the train any more, we sure as hell won't notice a rifle shot or two. Did it scare you?"

"No, no, not at all," I lied. "I just wondered where it came from. It's not the sort of thing you hear in the city."

"I guess not," Tom chuckled as he walked away, Kali bouncing around his feet. I turned back to the calmness of the lake, stretched, forgetting that I still had coffee dregs in the bottom of my cup, then swore as they dripped onto my face. It was time to face the real work of the day.

Still not hurrying, I wandered back to my cabin to pack some lunch supplies and the paperwork, did a quick run to the kitchen to fill my trusty thermos flask, then headed off down the road to the Netherby house. As soon as I left the sealed road, my driving became overly cautious as I hugged the edge, slowing for each corner, holding my breath till I was safely around the bend. By the time I turned into the Netherby gate I was exhausted. I pulled the car to a halt in front of the deck and relaxed back into the seat with a sigh of relief. In an instinctive motion, I reached into my pocket for my phone, then realised I hadn't thought about it all morning – a huge change from my city self who would have checked it every few minutes. It was still in the silent mode I had switched it to just before I had climbed into bed. I had been sure Simon would have called or sent texts and I was right. I noticed the five missed calls and deleted the texts without counting how many he had sent. Too many. I decided to leave the phone on silent. If someone important wanted to contact me, I could call them back. Simon I could do without.

As I braced myself to get out of the car and actually do some work, I remembered Gail's warning that Maggie Netherby had been a hoarder. Dreading what I was going to find, I climbed the steps to the deck, unlocked the door and threw it open. The house stank.

I clamped my hand over my mouth to hold back the stench that engulfed me, and bolted off the deck, swerving around my car, catching my hip on the fender as I dashed past in my rush to reach the boundary fence in time to be sick into the weeds. The fence post provided an uncomfortable prop as I bent over, eyes closed, breathing deeply, until the nausea went away and I could turn back to face the house. I needed a drink of water to take away the disgusting taste in my mouth but that would mean going inside. Leaning against the fence post in the fresh air seemed like a better idea, so for a while I stayed there, doing nothing, until the need for a drink forced me into action.

"Get a grip!" I spoke out loud, then automatically looked around to see who had heard me talking to myself, a habit I should have grown out of years ago. In the next paddock a sheep stared at me as if it agreed. I was right, though, I did need to get a grip; the house still needed to be sorted, so I needed to toughen up and go in. The stench needed to be dealt with and the sheep wasn't going to do it.

I straightened up, stretched and prepared for action, sizing up the distances between the door and the windows. My plan was to take a huge breath, run inside, open a window and run back out. One window at a time, then the French doors, then wait until the house had ventilated enough to venture inside. Surprisingly for me, as Simon always told me my plans were ill-conceived, it was a good plan, even when the window catches stuck and I was sure I was going to pass out before I got back to fresh air. When the house was open I slowed down, pulled my t-shirt up over my mouth and nose to lessen the smell, took a deep breath and stepped inside. It wasn't what I had expected.

At least half of the original villa had been converted into one large room. A modern kitchen filled one corner and a retro Formica dining table sat under the front windows, while the rest of the vast space was filled by an oversized, sagging lounge suite clustered around a huge log burner. Every wall was covered by bookcases, overflowing with books, magazines, random loose papers and quirky ornaments, It wasn't the cluttered hoard Gail had led me to expect but Margaret Netherby had a lot of belongings and the house still stank.

I retreated to the deck for air then tried again. The smell seemed to be coming from the kitchen. I flicked on the light switch beside the door to check an idea and the lack of response from the lights confirmed my suspicions. No power, therefore whatever had been left in the refrigerator had gone bad. The thought of clearing it out made me shudder. I retreated back to the deck to pluck up courage for the task.

Outside, the sound of an engine made me look up as a familiar dirty Land Rover pulled into the driveway.

I chose not to go down the steps to meet him, remembering instead another of Simon's body-language lessons about bosses having higher chairs to emit authority. From the deck I struck what I hoped was a pose that said don't mess with me - straight back, arms folded, looking down at him as he walked towards me. I didn't think he was fooled.

"Morning." His lopsided smile was tentative, as if he expected me to be angry, which made me suspicious.

"What brings you here?" I had no plans to let him off that easily, no matter how many muscles were hidden under the grubby Swanndri jacket.

"An apology."

I waited. We stared at each other. Finally he realised that we weren't playing conversation tag and it was still his turn.

"I really am sorry about yesterday, about the ditch. I wasn't being careful enough and I should have stopped to see if you were okay. In my defence, it really was an emergency. I really was in a hell of a hurry." He tried the lopsided smile again.

"Right. Well, thank you for stopping by, Mr Brown, but I need to find out what's rotten in this kitchen, so I don't have time to stop and chat."

"Oh, well, whatever. Have a good day then." He turned to leave. "By the way, my name's not Brown."

That threw me. Now it was my turn to apologise.

"Sorry. Tom at the campground called you Brownie, so I assumed your name was Brown."

He turned back, stepping up to my level on the deck, laughing.

"Tom's called me that since I was a kid. My name is actually Bruno, Bruno McTavish. And I gather you are Andrea North."

"Known as Andy, except to my ex, who not only insisted on Andrea but pronounced it On-dray-a." I held out my hand to shake his. "Pleased to meet you, Bruno McTavish, maybe we should pretend yesterday never happened and start again."

"I would like that."

The handshake went on just a little bit longer than politeness demanded, which was fine by me. It was Bruno who broke the moment with a sniff.

"Where is that smell coming from?"

"The kitchen, I think. I've been running backwards and forwards, holding my breath, trying to open the house up, and I am pretty sure it is coming from the fridge."

"Oh, gross! Hang on, I'll be back in a minute," Bruno jumped off the deck to rummage in the Land Rover. "Here," he waved something white in the air, "these might help. Face masks."

He sprinted back up the steps two at a time and handed me a flimsy piece of white fabric with an elastic strap. I was surprised that, coming out of his filthy vehicle, the mask was clean, then ashamed at myself for assuming it wouldn't be. With a murmured thanks, I held it to my face and pulled the elastic tight behind my head as he did the same. Nodding to each other, we simultaneously sucked in a lungful of fresh air and entered the house. I didn't need to lead Bruno to the kitchen, by his quick movements it was obvious that he knew the house layout well, so I followed and let him be the one to open the fridge door. Apart from a wilted lettuce, it was empty.

We looked at each other, miming confusion by flapping our hands. Bruno shrugged, then with a flick of his fingers, indicated he had thought of another place the smell could be coming from. At the back of the kitchen an open door led to a small room that would originally have been a bathroom but was now a spacious laundry, containing the largest freezer I had ever seen in a domestic house. Bruno hovered his hand over the lid, reluctant to open it. I nodded encouragement. He lifted the lid a few centimetres, which was quite enough to prove him right, then shut it quickly as the smell wafted out. We retreated outside where we could pull off the masks.

"Oh, that is just too disgusting," I said, watching the blond streaks in Bruno's hair glisten as he ran his hands through it in a way that was quite the opposite of disgusting.

"I don't even want to know what is in there," he answered. "I can guarantee one thing though, it won't be anything you need to account for on your asset list. Tell you what," he continued as I nodded in agreement, "let me give Tom a ring and see if he can come and give me a hand to get that freezer out of the house and onto my truck. Then I can take it to the dump. It's not like the freezer is salvageable. Let's just dump the whole lot."

"Good idea. I would appreciate that," I agreed. "I don't think I'm strong enough to help lift that thing, especially if it's full, and I don't intend to empty it unless I have to." Leaving him pulling out his phone, I decided to check out the rest of the house.

The remaining part of the original villa contained a plush master bedroom suite with a walk-in closet that must have once been a smaller bedroom and, on the other side, an extravagant bathroom in which ornate taps shaped like golden swans decorated a huge corner spa bath. I gave Margaret Netherby points for style, even if the end result was unfinished, the swans failing to conceal the unpainted plaster board on the walls and the lack of a door on the peach marble vanity unit. The luxury was still a work in progress.

I peeked into the walk-in wardrobe and wished it was mine. It was a closet to die for. A cleverly-designed system of racks and shelves covered three walls, with a full-length mirror and a pull-down ironing table, pulled down and permanently set up with an iron still plugged into the power but not switched on, taking up the space behind the door. Every rack was full of expensive, if old-fashioned, clothes while the shelves held an assortment of colourful hats with matching shoes and handbags. My idea of Margaret Netherby as a quaint country farmer blew out the window.

I retreated, shaking my head. I was still not seeing the proof that she was a hoarder. Why did Gail think she was, when the house was telling a different story? Maybe Bruno could give me more information. I found him back in the smelly laundry, attempting to move the freezer. He had taken off the Swanndri, so I was content to stand and watch his muscles flex as he struggled. Eventually he gave up, grinning as he noticed me watching.

"It's too much for me. I don't think it's budged an inch. Just as well help's on its way."

"Just as well. I thought you were going to burst

something."

"Yeah, so did I. I've always wondered why dead stuff is so much heavier than the same thing when it's alive. And I think there's a dead elephant in here."

"A dead, frozen elephant."

"Not frozen any more - if it was, it wouldn't smell so bad. Let's go outside and get some fresh air."

"Speaking of dead things," I said as I followed him through the lounge to the deck, "do you always carry dead pigs around or was yesterday a special treat?"

Bruno stopped and frowned back at me. "Yesterday was a sodding disaster!"

Suitably told off, I kept my thoughts to myself, at least until we got outside. Then I had to ask.

"So what do you do for a job that involves racing around the country with pigs, or taking time to move freezers? Are you a farmer or a pig hunter?"

I didn't get an answer as we were interrupted by the arrival of an ancient flat-deck truck followed by a pristine and expensive SUV. Tom and another older man clambered out of the truck, to be joined by two young men from the car. All four were clad in various colours of Swanndri, similar to Bruno's. Maybe the town got a bulk discount. Bruno greeted them all with much hand shaking and back slapping, then introduced them to me as Bob, Jake and Johnny, all apparently from the pub. I didn't ask if they owned it or just propped up the bar, instead I left them to work out how they were going to move the freezer and continued my perusal of the strange house.

Leading off the deck were two more bedrooms, both partially finished and sparsely decorated. One held a single wrought-iron bed covered by a handmade patchwork quilt while the other, the one with the best view down to the lake, contained nothing but a huge rocking chair with an accompanying side table holding a single book. The title surprised me. I hadn't been told much about Margaret Netherby and I certainly hadn't been told she was an author and an expert on wetlands.

Loud noises and colourful swear words drew me back to the laundry where the four men had succeeded in moving the freezer as far as the back steps. At least it was now outside the house, even if it was about to fall.

"For gawd's sake, don't let it go," Tom bellowed. "We don't want it to tip over and dump that shit here."

"Hold her right there," Bruno joined in. "Just keep it from slipping. Tom, we'll hang on here if you go and bring the truck around, Back it right up to the steps and we might be able to push it straight on."

Tom took off in a shambling run and soon his truck appeared around the side of the house. In a piece of precision driving, he turned the truck in the tight space and backed it to the steps in one move, then with a lot more swearing and grunting, the freezer was efficiently dragged on and secured with ropes. One of the young men, Jake or Johnny, I wasn't sure who was who, pulled a six-pack of beer seemingly out of nowhere and handed them around. I wasn't offered one.

"Cheers, mate," Bruno acknowledged the hard work by raising his beer as a toast. "Thanks, guys, I appreciate your help."

"She's right, mate," Bob replied on behalf of them all. "We'll get this down to the dump and you can get on with

your day."

"Yeah." Bruno looked at his watch. "Hell yeah. Amy'll be wondering where I've got to." He pulled his phone from his jean's pocket, checked it and grimaced. "Oh yeah, three missed calls. I'd better be going. Thanks again, guys." He flicked me a casual salute as he walked away. "Have a good rest of your day, Andrea North. I might catch you down at the pub later."

"Yeah, come and have a drink with us later," Bob agreed. "No, better than that, come to the pub for tea. We do a great venison pie."

I nodded, smiled and waved them goodbye without conscious thought because my brain was running an irritating loop. Amy. There's an Amy. An Amy who'll be wondering where he was. Damn. Who cares if there's an Amy? Why do I care that there's an Amy?

"Bugger Amy," I said to myself. "And bugger having no power in this place. I need a decent coffee."

I still hadn't asked Bruno, or Tom, why Gail had said Margaret was a hoarder so it was time to investigate the rest of the house – if I could figure out how to get into the other half. There were no doors off the passage that I hadn't opened and no doors off the lounge except the one onto the deck. I walked around the outside, looking carefully at where the two houses connected, then went through the rooms again, staring out windows to regain my bearings. It took a while but I worked it out. Margaret Netherby had a sense of humour. As, with a suitably ominous creak, a bookshelf pulled away from the wall to reveal a room, I realised that I would have liked Margaret. I wished I had the strength of character to be the sort of person who lived in a crazy house with a secret room, instead of being a downtrodden victim of a narcissistic bully. Maybe I could be. The days of being bullied were over. I wasn't sure what I was going to do after this job was finished, but why couldn't it include a crazy house that showed my personality? If I could remember what that was.

I found the hoard. The room was the original lounge of the cottage. From it, a passage led to two other rooms, both bare tongue and groove timber walls and both filled with cardboard boxes. I groaned. There was nothing on the boxes to suggest what was inside them, there were hundreds of them and they smelt bad. I could see mould growing on most of them and, when I stopped and stood still, I could hear mice. I groaned again, shuddered and backed away. The hoard could wait.

At least the smell of the rotten meat had mostly disappeared from the front of the house. Hopefully it would soon be clear enough to close some windows as I was getting cold, which made me think of electricity. I did a quick search of the obvious places and soon found a power bill, then pulled out my phone to have the power turned back on, which they promised to do, but not until tomorrow. For today there was no other option than to zip up my jacket and carry on.

My preliminary list divided Margaret's assets into categories including kitchen utensils, crockery, clothing, books and ornaments, all of which needed to be sorted into piles before I contacted the second-hand dealer who would value them for me. My second piece of paper listed the large furniture items, including the freezer to which I added a note saying it had been dumped as unsalvageable.

Once the furniture list was complete, I felt justified in stopping for the day. My watch told me it was almost mid-afternoon, which explained why I was hungry, and I desperately wanted to get warm. A venison pie in the pub sounded like a plan. With a quick final check on the rooms, I closed all the windows and locked the doors, justifying my leaving by telling myself that tomorrow the house wouldn't smell bad and would have power so I would have light and heat, and I could make as much coffee as I liked.

As I looked out from the deck, I realised there was something else I needed to check. On the other side of the parking area there was an old barn, divided into a garage, an open bay and an enclosed area with a huge door. The open bay held nothing but a few bales of hay, so I tried the garage. It took all my strength to drag open one side of the dilapidated double doors and, after the secret room, I should not have been as surprised as I was to be confronted by an immaculate vintage Studebaker, complete with running boards and gleaming headlamps.

"Wow!" I ran my hand over the fender. "What are you worth?"

I dragged the door shut, wondering why such a valuable car wasn't locked in, then did battle with the huge door on the third part of the barn, opening it just enough to see that it contained a large workbench and an assortment of metal tools that I couldn't identify. I would add them to the list of things to ask the second-hand dealer to help me with.

In the car, I turned up the heat and the radio, singing along to an old country song as I drove back to Waihola. By the time I parked beside my cabin I was warm again but my stomach was starting to rumble from the lack of lunch, so I threw my paperwork onto my bed, locked the door and set off for the pub.

Bob was right. The venison pie was sensational, served with roast potatoes and pumpkin and washed down with a Speights beer. I found a small table over by the window so I could enjoy watching the view while I ate, but I didn't object to being joined by Jake and Johnny, who turned out to be brothers. While Bob ran the bar, they propped it up as I discovered they actually worked at the service station over the road, which was owned by their father. I was still finding it difficult to work out who was who as they interrupted each other's sentences so often I felt like I was talking to one person in two bodies. My plan, when they joined me, was to quiz them about Bruno, not that I cared about him, and find out more about Amy, not that I cared about her either, but they had an agenda of their own.

"What are you going to do with the dog?" the one I thought was Jake asked.

"What? Kali the pug? Why? What's she done?"

"Not Kali. Maggie Netherby's dog. What's going to happen to him?"

"I didn't know she had a dog. There's no mention of it in the paperwork. And I didn't see a dog at the house. Where is it?"

"At the pound," Johnny answered. "We've asked them if we can take him, but the dog ranger says we don't have any official proof we are allowed to take him. Which is just stupid because Maggie's dead. She can't write us a letter saying it's okay for us to look after her dog. And nobody else seems to care about him. Can you do something? He'll be put down otherwise and he's a really nice dog."

It was the longest speech one of them had made without the other joining in, showing me how serious they were. Jake was furiously nodding his agreement.

"Yeah, we don't want to just leave him there. Can you help?"

"All right." I agreed. "Get me all the details on who I need to speak to and I will contact them."

The J brothers rose together then soon returned to hand me a piece of paper with a phone number scrawled on it in green ink.

"That's the pound's number. Tell them it's okay for us to pick him up."

I gave them the sort of nod that looks like agreement but doesn't promise anything, tucking the paper into my pocket as I thanked them again for their help with the freezer.

"No problem," they said in unison.

"Happy to help", one said while the other said, "Sing out if you need us again," at exactly the same time. I still couldn't tell them apart, but I liked Jake and Johnny.

A dog. Now I had to deal with a dog.

I finished my meal, walked back to my cabin and checked the paperwork. There was no mention of a dog. With a sigh, I dialled the pound's number, wondering as I did so what kind of dog Maggie Netherby would have. It would be either a tiny handbag dog or a giant hairy thing, although logic said it would was probably a sheepdog. When the phone went to an answering machine telling me the pound had closed for the day, I flicked it off, promising myself I would try again in the morning. So why did I feel guilty?

I made a few more phone calls to the dealers and valuers our firm preferred to work with, making appointments with two of them to value the furniture and the books, then I closed the folder and deliberately turned it upside down. Work was finished for the day. Outside the sky was beginning to darken, casting an ethereal gloom over the lake. I pulled my jacket back on, drawn by the gentle rhythmic lapping of the water against the shoreline.

I drew up my hood against the chilly southerly wind, shoved my hands deep into my pockets and tried to pretend it was summer as I wandered along the lakeshore, charmed, as always, by the antics of the scaups. Further out several swan couples floated, holding their place against the pull of the tide, ignoring the mallard ducks fishing for food. A shout from behind alerted me to the presence of the rushing pug just before she ran past, heading for the water.

"Kali! Come back here!" Gail called, unheeded by the little dog who ran out onto the wooden jetty and threw herself into the water. I laughed.

"Damn," Gail cursed as she joined me. "I was hoping to catch her before she got wet."

"Too late."

"Yep. Damn!" We waited for the dog to surface. "What the hell is she bringing in this time?"

We swore in unison when we saw what Kali was dragging ashore from under the jetty.

Chapter 3

I admit I was completely useless. All I could do was stare in disbelief at the object hanging from the pug's mouth. I muttered several inane profanities. I used the F word a lot, mixed with a few oh-my-gods and what-the-hells. But I didn't actually do anything. Surely it was a fake. Gail, however, launched into action. She scooped up the soaking wet dog, trying to avoid touching the disgusting thing in Kali's mouth, and shook her, yelling, "Drop it! Drop it!" as she struggled to get the dog to give up her prize. Finally, after what seemed like hours but was probably only a few seconds, Kali obeyed, confused by the angry reaction to her latest toy. The forearm and hand flopped onto the grass.

"What the f...?" I said one more time.

Gail kept a tight grip on the wet, squirming donor of the gift and took command.

"Have you got your cell phone on you?"

I nodded, sensible words failing to form.

"Then get it out and call triple one – get the police down here. Then stay here. I'm going to take Kali back to the house and shut her in and I'll bring Tom back with me. Don't let anyone touch anything while I'm away."

I nodded again, even though I thought the advice was unnecessary. The German tourists were still out on the road somewhere and I didn't think the swans were going to rush out of the water to steal the thing. There was no way I was going to pick it up. I kept nodding as Gail rushed off, then did as she had ordered. The emergency call was answered promptly but I knew that the police would have to come either from Balclutha or Dunedin, so I assumed I would be waiting a while before they showed up.

I was mistaken. I heard someone coming and looked around, expecting to see Gail and Tom, who were running towards me at Tom's top speed. Just ahead of them, though, at an angle that suggested he had run from the pub, another figure pounded across the grass, overtaking them and reaching me first. In his casual jeans and rugby shirt I didn't recognise him as a policeman, so I stepped forward with my hand up to stop him.

"Woah! You can't jog here at the moment, sorry. You'll have to go another way."

"Do I look daft enough to be a jogger?" the newcomer panted. "You must be Andrea North? I'm Senior Sergeant Ian Carlton." He pulled an identification card out of his pocket and flashed it at me. "Sorry, I'm not actually on duty. I was up at the pub, we'd just finished rugby practice down at the domain," he pointed towards the far end of the lake where the campground ended and the council-owned common land opened into a park, "but I'm the man on the spot so they gave me a call. What's the problem?"

"That." I gestured to the arm still lying where Kali had dropped it. "Gail's pug retrieved it from under the jetty."

"Oh. Right." Senior Sergeant Carlton looked as revolted as I was. "It's an arm."

"Good guess."

"I mean, it's a human arm."

I desperately wanted to say, "No shit, Sherlock," but I bit my tongue. "Well, it's not a swan's leg," was the best I came up with.

"It could be rubber. Some kind of Halloween prop." Carlton's hopeful look was quickly quashed by Gail as she puffed up with Tom at her heels.

"Don't be ridiculous." She waited for a reaction that didn't come. "Well, go on then," she pushed Carlton towards the arm, "take a closer look. Is it a fake or is it real?

Carlton looked around for a plausible escape route, found none, remembered that he was the official with the badge and reluctantly peered down at the arm and hand.

"Okay," he agreed with a grimace, "It's real. Look, I'm going to have to call this in then rope this area off. Can you guys please wait here while I get some stuff out of my car?"

"We can get our stories straight while he's away," Tom said, casually rolling himself a cigarette while Carlton ran back towards the pub.

"What stories?" Gail asked. "And don't light that up, this is a crime scene, you idiot."

"Our alibis." Tom's smile gave him away. "You know, how we were all together when the pug murdered whoever it was and gnawed his arm off."

"Oh, for heaven's sake, don't be so stupid!"

"Sorry, love, but if, as you said, this is a crime scene, shouldn't he have taken our statements, or whatever they do, before he ran off? Or do they only do that on tv?"

"Well I don't know, do I? It's not like Kali finds bits of bodies every day. Anyway, who is it?"

"Hard to tell," said Tom. "Bugger all there to tell by. What's that around his wrist?"

"How do you know it's a him?" I forced myself to have another look at the pale thing flopped on the ground in front of us.

Tom shrugged. "I don't, really. It just kind of looks like a man's hand. I'd expect a lady's hand to be smaller. But I could be wrong. But what is that around the wrist?" He stepped forwards, bending over to peer at the object without touching it or getting too close. Gail and I did the same but the cylinder of carved wood tied around the wrist by a band of plaited leather meant nothing to me.

"It's a duck caller." Tom said, straightening up. "And what's more, I think it's Gunna's."

"Gunna?" Gail gasped. "Are you telling me that's Gunna's arm?"

"I hope not, but I know his fancy duck caller when I see it, and I can't see him lending it to anyone else. Anyway," he put his arm around Gail and squeezed her in a comforting hug, "let's leave it to them and let them work it out."

We all turned to see who he was talking about, Gail leaning against her husband as we watched Ian Carlton's police car drive slowly around the lake edge towards us. Gail and Tom talked quietly to themselves about the arm but I watched Senior Sergeant Carlton with interest as he busied himself wrapping official tape around the jetty. He was good looking in a different way to Bruno the pig-man. While Bruno had the "Southern Man" look of hard muscles on a wiry, slender frame, Ian Carlton was the opposite. His rugby jersey strained across broad shoulders, bulging biceps stretching the sleeves as he pulled the tape tightly around convenient trees.

"Right, that should hold it," he said as he tied the tape's end to the jetty railing. "Now we wait for the boss and the others to get here. Any chance of a cup of coffee, Gail?"

"Yeah, good idea," said Tom, moving his wife away from

where she had been leaning on him. "We could all do with a hot cuppa. Thanks, love."

"I'll help," I offered. "It's better than staring at that thing."

Gail nodded, meekly allowing me to lead her towards the house where Kali's excited greeting shook her out of her bewilderment.

"Oh, you silly, silly dog," she said as she filled the jug and switched it on. "Whatever have you got us into? Who have you found? And where is the rest of him?"

"Who is this Gunna you think it might be?" I asked as Gail spooned instant coffee into mismatched mugs.

"Gunna? Tom knows more about him than I do. All I know is that he's some kind of loner hermit bloke who hangs around the lake watching the birds. Doesn't seem to do anything else. He was a friend of that Maggie Netherby you're sorting out. He spent a lot of time at her place. That's where he got the nickname Gunna."

"Why? Is he into guns or something?"

"Ask Tom when we get this coffee down to them. He likes telling that story."

I was intrigued but it was obvious I would have to wait so, forcing patience I didn't have, I wrangled four coffee cups while Gail convinced Kali she wasn't coming with us then relieved me of two of the cups. With reservations about what we were returning to, we picked our way through the moonlit darkness back to the jetty, the waiting men and the severed arm.

"Tom," I said as I handed him his coffee, "Gail said to ask you why Gunna is called Gunna. Has it got anything to do with guns?"

"No, not at all," Tom laughed. "It came from that Netherby place you're here to organise. You've seen the house – it's a right jigsaw of a place. Two houses stuck together. Lots of potential, as the land agents would say, but lots of work to get it finished. Maggie did what she could but Gunna was the handyman. His real name's Harry, Harold I suppose, but he quickly got called Gunna when he was at the pub, always telling everyone what his grand plans were for the place. He was always going to do this, going to do that. You get it?" He looked at me but I shook my head. Whatever he was putting down, I wasn't picking up. He explained. "Going to – gunna – gunna do this, gunna do that."

"Oh!" I laughed. "I get it."

"Yep. The funny thing is, he never did anything he said he was gunna do. Which is why the nickname stuck."

"And you reckon that's his arm?" the policeman interrupted, pointing to the flaccid lump on the ground.

"Never said that," Tom denied. "But I am pretty sure that's his duck caller around that wrist."

"So, while we're waiting," Carlton turned to me, "tell me what happened."

I told him about walking down to the foreshore, then watching Kali leap into the water, only to come out clutching the arm in her mouth. Gail added her piece, adding how Kali had run ahead of her. We both agreed we hadn't seen the arm floating in the lake until the dog brought it out. Carlton asked me how much I knew about Gunna to which I replied that I knew absolutely nothing.

"I hadn't heard of him until Tom mentioned his name when he saw that thing on the wrist there."

"So why are you in Waihola anyway?" Carlton asked.

"Funny time of year for a holiday."

"No, I'm here for work. I'm an estate executor and I am here to value and document the assets of the late Margaret Netherby so her property can be sold. I've been up at her property all day today – it's going to be a bigger task than I expected."

"You found the hoard?" Gail grinned.

"Yes, I did. Thanks for the warning. It would have been a bit of a shock if I hadn't been looking for it. The front of the house is so beautiful, the back was certainly a surprise."

Yeah," Tom agreed. "Gunna was always gunna sort it out, gunna make shelves, gunna file it all neatly. Yeah, right!"

"Hoard? Hoard of what?" Carlton asked me, but before I could answer him the headlights of two cars and a large van lit the scene as they drove over the grass towards us. Carlton thrust his empty cup into my hands and strode forwards to meet them.

All of a sudden the quiet lake front felt more like the summer holidays. There seemed to be people rushing everywhere, erecting a tent over the arm, taking photographs, even measuring things on the ground that I couldn't even see. Somebody wearing waist-high fishing waders was walking into the water, shining a flashlight under the jetty. I guessed they were looking for the rest of the body. I stood with Gail and Tom, none of us knowing what we were supposed to do next, but when nobody came to talk to us, the novelty of the police action was soon overtaken by the realisation that I was cold. I told them that I was going back to my cabin, knowing that from there I would be able to watch the action in more comfort. I handed Gail the empty cups I had been clutching and set off, taking a wide loop around the scurrying police team, but I hadn't got far before Carlton's voice stopped me in my tracks.

"Oi! You can't just wander off. We need to speak to you."

I swung round, standing my ground as he strode towards me.

"Well, you've had plenty of opportunity. I've been standing here, freezing my butt off for," I glanced at my watch, "nearly 45 minutes and nobody's bothered to talk to any of us."

I was starting to enjoy the new, confidant, post-Simon me but I don't think Senior Sergeant Carlton shared my enjoyment. His face muscles and his fists tensed as he fought back an angry retort that was never delivered as another voice called out, "Sorry. If you want to wait where it's warmer, I'll be with you shortly."

"Okay," I called back to the kneeling figure I could barely make out in the gloom, "I'll be in my cabin. It's the first one in the block."

Carlton's glare stabbed my shoulder blades as I walked away.

It wasn't much warmer in my cabin, so I was huddled on the bed, wrapped up in a blanket, when the voice arrived and introduced himself by handing me a business card and settling himself comfortably on the end of the bed. He told me his name was Harris and his rank was detective, although he looked more like an accountant, or a benevolent school teacher. He ran his hands through thinning hair, then slapped his arms for warmth in the chilly cabin.

"Well," he said, pulling a notebook and pen from the pocket of his well-worn windjacket, "I will start by apologising for leaving you standing out there in the cold.

Miss North, is it? But I think you'd agree, it's not a situation we come across every day. So, I know you've already told Senior Sergeant Carlton, but can you please run me through the details again. How did you happen to pull an arm out of the lake?"

"I didn't. Kali the pug did. I was just walking down to the lake when she dashed past me, with Gail in hot pursuit. She leapt into the lake, swan under the jetty, then came back out, carrying that thing in her mouth. I thought it was a tree branch until she brought it right up to us."

"What did you do then?"

"Umm, I think I swore a lot, we both did, then Gail made her drop it and I rang the police because I had my cell phone in my pocket. Gail took Kali back to the house and I waited with the .. the thing."

"So when did you recognise who it belonged to?"

"What? I didn't recognise it. What are you talking about?"

Harris looked up from the notebook he had been scribbling in.

"Harold Stevens." He stared at me, waiting for my answer. I stared back, waiting for his explanation. As the silence became a deadlock, I shook my head.

"I have no idea who you are talking about. Who is Harold Stevens and why do you think I would recognise his arm?"

"Carlton said you were all talking about him. So which one of you recognised the arm as his?"

I shook my head more. "We weren't talking about any Harold Stevens. Tom was telling me about some guy called Gunna." I facepalmed my hand to my forehead as I suddenly understood. "Oh, Gunna. Is Harold Stevens his proper name?"

"Yes, it gather Stevens is known locally as Gunna. So it was Tom who identified the arm as belonging to Stevens?"

"No."

"But you just said..."

"No," I interrupted. "Tom recognised and identified the duck caller tied around the wrist, but he very firmly said that it didn't prove it was Gunna's arm. His duck caller, yes; his arm, maybe."

Harris just nodded and scribbled in his book.

"Did you think it looked like Gunna's arm?"

"Oh, for heaven's sake!" I exploded up off the bed. "How the hell would I know what Gunna's arm looks like? I only arrived here yesterday! I've never clapped eyes on the man. I wouldn't know him from a bar of soap!"

Harris sat back, raising his hands protectively over his face in his surprise at my outburst, then lowering them to pat the bed, which I took as an invitation to sit down again. I remained standing.

"My apologies. I have completely misunderstood Senior Sergeant Carlton," Harris said.

"Why? Did he say I knew the man? What other rubbish has he told you?"

'No, no. Please sit down." He patted the bed again. "He said you were working at the Netherby place, so I assumed you had met Stevens."

"Why would you assume that?" I sat back down on the bed and pulled the blanket tighter around my shoulders.

"Because, according to Carlton, Stevens lives out there, on the edge of the lake, in a caravan."

"Oh. That's news to me. There's nothing about him in any of the information I have been given."

"So you haven't seen him hanging around?"

"No. So far the only people I have met are Tom and Gail, two young guys from the garage across the road and the guy from the pub – and only because they helped me move a stinky freezer out of the house. Oh, and some pig hunter called Bruno who drives like an idiot."

"He's worse than an idiot, he's a troublemaker," Carlton's voice came through the door before him. "Take my advice and have as little as possible to do with him." Ignoring my open mouth and indrawn breath as I prepared my response, he faced the detective, "They're just about done, Sir, but they want to check with you before they take the arm away."

My mouth was still preparing to speak as he turned away and melted back into the darkness. Harris rose, running his fingers through his hair as he had when he'd arrived.

"Thank you, Miss North. I will be in touch. I presume you will be here if we need you again?"

"Here in the evenings, or at the Netherby house during the day. I was hoping the job would only take a day or two but it may take all week, judging from what I saw in the house yesterday. There could be a lot more to sort than I expected."

Harris thrust his notebook back into his jacket pocket, pulled his collar up and departed.

From the doorway, blanket wrapped tightly to keep out the cold, I watched the two men. Harris had caught up to Carlton and they had stopped to talk. I couldn't hear what they were saying but by the body language I could guess that the older, smaller man was giving orders and Carlton was taking them. They parted company and my eyes followed Carlton as he strode towards his car, his muscles rippling under his rugby shirt. The cold forced me to close my door, but I wondered if I would see him again in the morning. In my head I ran through a series of questions I could use to strike up a conversation with him, then discarded them all as pathetic. I mentally told myself off. I had just successfully walked away from a domineering partner, so why was I hankering after the first set of broad shoulders I had met? But, unable to resist, I peeked out of the window and could barely make him out in the darkness, leaning against his car. I thought about taking him a cup of coffee but it was too cold and dark to venture over to the communal kitchen, so I just watched him for a while through the window. Eventually he walked away, talking into his mobile phone. I took that as my cue to go to bed. As I relaxed, I admitted to myself that I found this policeman attractive and that I really did hope I would see him in the morning. At least I could ask him what trouble Bruno had caused.

Chapter 4

He wasn't there in the morning. I slept late, so the sun was shining when I finally stuck my head out of the cabin door. Down at the lakefront, it was surprisingly quiet. I had expected to see a swarm of people still buzzing around doing whatever they had been doing when I went to bed, but they had all decamped sometime during the night, leaving only one bored constable in uniform guarding the tape that fluttered in the light breeze. I was tempted to ask him if they had worked out whose arm we had found but I was hungry, so I settled for grabbing my supplies and scampering across to the kitchen, acutely aware that I was still wearing my pyjamas.

Fortunately for my ego, the kitchen was empty. The German tourists had packed their campsite and continued their journey, saving me from the embarrassment of facing them dressed in pink flannelette. Unfortunately, my sense of relief didn't last long. I had made my toast, smothered it with jam and taken a huge, satisfying bite when the kitchen door opened behind me. I spun around to be faced with Tom but it was the person behind him I noticed first. I chewed my toast quickly, swallowing fast as my face went as red as the raspberry jam. Bruno's eyes travelled from my dishevelled hair, past my flushed cheeks to the silver unicorn embroidered on my pyjama top. The girl who had just escaped from a bully flinched inside me, waiting for the harsh rebuke that never came.

"Good morning." A laugh instead of a lecture. "Slept in,

did we?"

"Well, I might have, but you obviously didn't," I retorted. How dare he use "we" when he meant me. We were not conjoined twins. "But then I guess you weren't up till all hours finding a piece of human, then dealing with annoying police who expected you to know who it was."

"No, no I wasn't. I was sleeping like a baby through all your excitement. I didn't know anything about it until Tom told me this morning."

"Gail sent me to check you were all right," Tom interjected, just before I had thought of a suitably caustic reply.

"And I just happened to turn up at the right time, so I joined him." Bruno flashed me a smile I did not return, even though my heart rate quickened. I took another bite of toast to cover what I hoped was not another blush.

"Are you all right?" Tom asked. "Did you get any sleep at all with all those police? Gail was watching them out the window till all hours. Better than the tv, she reckoned."

"Yes, I got to sleep after the detective and Sergeant Carlton had gone," I said, not expecting the angry growl that came from Bruno.

"Carlton? Was he here? Bastard!"

"Yeah, he said nice things about you, too," I replied.

"I bet he did. Don't trust him. Don't trust anything he says or does."

"That's pretty much what he said about you. I gather you two are old friends then?"

"Huh! Yeah, maybe, back when we were at primary school. Then he grew up and became a prick."

"Why? Because he became a policeman and gave you too

many fines for bad driving?"

I could see Bruno stifle the swear words he wanted to reply with, before he exhaled a long breath, shook his head and turned to Tom.

"Boy, she sure does hold a grudge, doesn't she?" He turned back to me and tugged his floppy, blond-streaked forelock, bowing as he did so. "Well, Miss North, I can see that you are just fine, so I will be on my way. I hope you have a pleasant day. Catch you later at the pub, Tom."

"Yep, I'll pay you for that pig."

"I'd better be going too," I said. "I've got a lot to do today and I'm already late."

"Late? You're not on a clock, don't worry about it."

"You're right, Tom, but old habits die hard and all that. I'm so used to office hours I feel guilty standing around in my pyjamas when I should be working. Actually, I feel guilty standing around in my pyjamas at all, especially in public, so I think I will take my toast and go find some clothes."

Tom laughed as I gathered my breakfast things.

"Sing out if you want a hand to sort through Maggie Netherby's stuff. I think Gail would love an excuse to find out what's in that hoard. Maggie certainly kept it well hidden. Gail has all sorts of theories about what's up there."

"Gail might get her wish. I've only had a brief look but there are two rooms full of boxes and I think I am going to need someone to help me go through them or I'll be here all year." I looked out the door towards the lake. "Not that staying here longer would be a bad thing. Waihola is just as lovely as I remembered."

I hurried back to my cabin and pulled on my jeans, my one clean t-shirt and my warm jersey. Non-office clothes to go with my non-office hours. I unplugged my phone from its charger and checked my emails. There was nothing from Simon. No emails, no texts. Had he finally got the message that I wasn't coming back? I hoped so. As I drove away, I started to make lists in my head of what I had to achieve. I decided to start by completing the inventory of the lived-in rooms, then take a look at the garage and sheds before I tackled the secret rooms. I would need to contact someone to value the vintage car. The thought of the car, just as I paused opposite the garage, waiting to turn onto the main highway, jogged my memory. I had to sort out the dog and I should do that first. I would go into Mosgiel and find the dog pound, then I could sign any paperwork needed to let them release the dog to the J brothers. I glanced down at my clothes. I could also find a shop and buy more clothes. I might be here a while.

I found the shopping mall before I found the dog pound so it was almost lunch time before I fronted up to the white, austere desk in the pound's reception area and rang the bell as the note beside it instructed me to do. A pleasant-faced woman in an official khaki uniform entered through a side door after a few minutes, apologising for keeping me waiting. I explained who I was and why I was there, only to be astounded by her reply.

"If I had any other options left, there is no way in hell those boys would get Jackson!"

"Jackson? Is that the dog's name? And why not? They seem nice boys and very keen to give him a home. I presume he's a him, if that's his name."

"Yes, he's called Jackson. And yes, they are not bad boys, but ...."

"But what?"

"Because they want him as a hunting dog, not a pet, and that leaves me with an awful dilemma. He's not a hunting dog, or even an outside dog. He's a house dog. He's never slept in an outside kennel in his life. Do you know anything about him?"

"No, only what I was told by the J brothers. He's not mentioned in any of the information I was given."

"Okay. Jackson is a retired show dog. A grand champion, actually. He's a gentle, sweet boy who has been pampered. And he's not young any more. He's nine years old. So, even if we are supposed to be happy with anyone willing to take on one of our unclaimed dogs, in Jackson's case putting him down is a better option than letting him suffer in the wrong hands. You'll understand when you meet him. Follow me."

I was going to argue that I was just happy to sign any papers she needed signed but those words "putting him down" didn't sit well. I followed her. She led me through a side door past two rows of wire cages in which dogs of all shapes and sizes barked noisily as we approached. At the very end of the second row, she stopped and pointed dramatically at a pile of blankets in the back of a cage.

"Um?" I couldn't see a dog.

"Jackson," the ranger called softly. "Jackson, come on boy."

The blankets moved. A long, pointed nose twitched, followed by a long, skinny leg. The blankets rose, then fell to the floor as a tan and white dog emerged, his soulful, dark eyes begging for attention as he walked slowly towards us, his tail almost wagging in hopeful anticipation.

"Oh my god," I breathed. "He's gorgeous. But I thought

greyhounds were bigger than that."

"They are. He's not a greyhound, he's a whippet. As I said, I don't know what to do. His time is up and the boys are the only ones interested in adopting him, but... oh, I just wish... could you take him?"

I formed in my head all the reasons why I couldn't. I live in Wellington. Jackson tilted his head and stared at me. I live in an apartment. Jackson wagged his tail. I'm only in Otago for a few days, maybe a week. Jackson stood on his hind legs, pressing his nose against the wire gate. He whined. A tiny, pleading, almost soundless cry. I looked into his huge brown eyes.

"Yes," I said.

Ten minutes later Jackson was snuggled in his blanket on the back seat of my car, the ranger waving him goodbye as I drove away. I now owned a dog. Simon would be furious.

When I reached the Netherby house I pulled the blanket off Jackson's head and gave him a reassuring pat.

"Come on, boy, you're home. Let's go inside."

He clambered out of the car, wandered sedately to the nearest tree to lift his leg, then climbed the steps to the front door. As soon as I unlocked it, he headed straight for the couch where he settled down and promptly went back to sleep. I gave him another pat then went in search of the electric jug. I needed coffee. I prayed that a miracle had happened while I was away and electricity had been restored and my prayers were answered. The light on the jug glowed when I flicked the switch. Yes! Jackson's raised head made me realise I had said that aloud. Amazing how a twitch of a dog's ears could make a person feel embarrassed. A quick search of her pantry showed me that Maggie Netherby had a gourmet taste in coffee, with several jars of a fancy brand in different flavours. I justified drinking the hazelnut one on the grounds that all the opened foods would be thrown out, so drinking it was acceptable as a perk of the job. Then it was back to business.

Piece by piece I worked my way through Maggie Netherby's ornaments, books and personal effects, noting and counting every one, until a whine from Jackson made me realise that it was starting to get dark. Earlier I had found a dog lead hanging behind the laundry door, so I attached it to the wide, hand-tooled leather collar he was wearing, pulled on my jacket and told Jackson we were going for a walk. He led the way, taking me to the fence, beyond which was a paddock with a magnificent view over the lake. Even though the light was fading, I clambered through the wire and let the dog take me across the field to the opposite boundary where, although he wanted to keep going, I stopped to lean on the fence.

"No, Jackson, that's far enough. Time to go back. What's that down there, though?"

I don't know why I expected a dog to answer me but I was intrigued. The paddock merged into lake edge, the grass giving way to reed patches as the solid land became a tidal zone. In the dusk I could make out a shape that looked like some kind of small building which, as I peered at it, seemed to have a faint light moving inside it. Then the light was gone. I shook my head.

"I must be imagining things," I said to the dog. "Come on, let's go back where it's warm. I saw some cans of dog food in the pantry so let's get ourselves some food."

Food was obviously a magic word as Jackson wagged his

tail and let me lead him back to the house where I opened a can of dog food and tipped it into the bowl I had found earlier in a kitchen cupboard. I watched him gulp it down, then realised I was just as hungry as he was, so I decided to pack up for the day and return to the motor camp. But what would I do with the dog? Even though the house was his home, I couldn't leave him by himself, that just seemed wrong. I had signed the papers so I owned him now. From now on I had to include him in my plans. I sat down on a dining chair with a thump as the reality hit me. I liked him. When the ranger had asked me to take him, I had thought I would just look after him until I could find him a new home. I saw him as another chattel I had to organise. But in just a few hours his big eyes and quiet nature had got to me. I had no idea how I was going to manage with him in Wellington but I had to make it work. I would worry about that later. For tonight I hoped Gail would be fine with Jackson at the motor camp. I guessed she would be.

I guessed right. When I told Gail the story, she was happy to let him share my cabin.

"Strictly, it's against health regulations, so don't let too many people see him. I won't say anything. I won't even tell Tom, it can be our secret. I remember Jackson, he was in the show ring the same time Kali was."

"Kali? A show dog?"

"Hard to believe now, isn't it?" Gail laughed. "Yes, believe it or not, that fat blob is a show champion. Not as flash as Jackson but she did all right in her day. Maggie Netherby was well known in the circuit. Jackson was the last of a long string of prize winners. I'm glad you've got him. Are you going to keep him?"

"I wasn't going to but I'm getting far too attached to him, far too quickly. I will have to look for a new place to live when I go back to Wellington but ...," I paused to shrug my shoulders, "I needed a complete change, so maybe Jackson will be just the catalyst I need to make it happen."

Later, after I had heated myself a tasteless but instant meal, Gail and I walked our dogs down to the lake, both firmly controlled on their leads as I was afraid Jackson would run away because I hadn't worked out yet how obedient he was and Gail was afraid Kali would dive into the water and drag out the rest of the body. The police tape still flapped from the edge of the jetty but all other signs of the previous night's activity had disappeared, a few tyre tracks the only proof anything had happened. As we walked, we talked about the arm and who it could belong to, with Gail saying that the popular opinion was on Gunna as he hadn't been seen for over a week.

"Is that unusual?" I asked.

"Yeah. He might go a few days without anyone seeing him, but he didn't turn up at the pub last Friday and that's way out of character. He likes his beers, does Gunna. He's always there on Friday nights."

The dogs were pulling on their leads, so we mutually decided to leave the jetty and our speculations. Gail let Kali drag her back towards her house and Jackson high-stepped beside me as I turned towards my cabin.

Jackson beat me to bed, worming his way under the blanket down to the bottom, but then he didn't have pyjamas to get into or a phone to check and put on charge. There was a text from Simon headed *Open this*. So I did. I read it out loud, imitating his pompous, demanding tone, including his ridiculous pronunciation of my name.

"On-dray-a." God forbid that he should ever shorten it to Andy. Far too common. "I expect you to be back here for Mother's birthday dinner tomorrow evening. Wear the blue calf-length dress with the silver belt. Silver shoes."

"Well, let me think," I answered aloud as I deleted the message. "Um, no. One, I hate you. Two, I hate your mother. Three, I am busy here and four, the dress is somewhere in an op-shop by now. Tough luck." Jackson wriggled his head out of bed to see who I was talking to, so I gave him a pat. "You would save me from Simon Bastard, wouldn't you? Let me into bed. You're a much nicer bed-mate than he ever was." I snuggled in beside him, enjoying his warmth as he curled into my arms while we drifted off to sleep.

The gunshots woke us up.

Jackson reacted first, leaping out of bed, dragging the blanket with him.

"It's okay," I soothed, hauling the blanket back onto the bed and patting it to entice Jackson back. "Come on, boy."

Then, another three shots in quick succession. Jackson's ears pricked forwards, towards the lake. I shot out of bed, automatically reaching for Jackson and crouching down on the floor. I could see that he wanted to investigate but there was no way I was going outside. I stayed kneeling at his level, stroking him as he fretted with the same soft, worried whine he had given me at the dog pound. We were both shivering.

"It's probably those rat shooters again," I told Jackson in an effort to convince myself. "At the dump. It sounded a lot closer than that though, didn't it. You thought so too. Whatever it was, there's nothing we can do about it. Let's go back to bed."

I must have sounded more confident than I felt because Jackson stopped shivering and jumped back into bed. With no real options, I followed, straightening the blanket as best as I could but, although Jackson went out like a light, I found real sleep impossible. I tossed and turned with intermittent patches of weird dreams involving Simon in a dress and carrying a shotgun, chasing me through a large, abandoned house. I would get to a part where I entered a lavishly furnished room full of brocade-covered furniture, then just before his mother, who was sitting in a large wing-backed chair, turned to face me, I would wake up, toss, turn and repeat the whole thing again. At five thirty when the darkness of the night began to lighten into daybreak, I gave up trying to sleep and got up. I pulled on my jacket over my pyjamas, grabbed Jackson's lead and yanked the blanket back to get his attention.

"Come on, lazy bones. Let's go for a walk."

We sauntered slowly down to the lake front, past the jetty with its flapping crime scene tape, stopping at every bush for Jackson to mark his territory. We had gone a reasonable distance when I realised that there was a vehicle parked near the boat ramp. The man beside it was picking things off the ground and throwing them onto its deck. I turned Jackson around and went the other way. It was too early in the morning to get into polite conversation with the rubbish collector and after Gail's warning, I didn't want to have to explain the presence of my dog. I had a vague feeling that something about the man looked familiar but he was too far away to see properly, so I shrugged it off. Who cared anyway?

I left Jackson in the cabin, tucked under the blanket

again, while I had a shower then made myself some breakfast toast and coffee. It's a funny thing about memory, strange little things trigger it. It was the toast. As soon as I took a bite, I remembered yesterday's embarrassing breakfast encounter and I knew exactly who I had seen at the boat ramp. Bruno. What had he been picking up that early in the morning? Again I shrugged off the thought. Really, it was no business of mine. Maybe picking up rubbish was part of his job. I never did find out what he did with his time. I took another bite of toast and decided to check my phone. Yes, there was another text from Simon.

I have booked you on the 10.25 a.m. flight.

Damn! Now I would have to ring the airport and tell them not to expect me, otherwise they would be holding up the flight and yelling my name incoherently over the loudspeakers, because there was no way I was going to be on it. I found and dialled the airport's number, then held while they connected me to the airline counter. I was honest, explaining that I had got away from an abusive ex and that, no matter how much he spent, I wasn't flying back to him to go to his mother's birthday party. The girl on the phone laughed, cancelled my ticket then regretfully informed me that Simon wouldn't get a refund, which made me laugh in return.

Harbouring pleasantly revengeful thoughts of how pissed off Simon would be when I didn't alight from the plane, I hurried back to my cabin to pack Jackson and my bag into the car for an early start at the Netherby house. A quick check of the fuel gauge suggested a brief stop at the garage for petrol. As I pulled in beside the petrol pumps, I noticed a vehicle partially hidden around the side of the building. I recognised it instantly. Bruno. I couldn't see him inside so I moved quickly, hoping to get my petrol before he appeared. Then he did, walking to the back of his Land Rover and reaching into the deck. As he pulled out two dead swans I gasped in horror. That was what he had been loading at the boat ramp. And that explained the gunshots. Bruno had been shooting swans in the dead of night, then retrieving them when it got light enough to find them in the reeds. I was revolted. He had seemed so nice when he helped me with the freezer, but he really was the disgusting animal killer I had first thought he was. Dead pigs now dead swans. I wanted nothing more to do with Bruno McTavish.

He disappeared again around the back of the building so I quickly finished my transaction, grateful that the pay-at-the-pump option meant I didn't have to go inside, heaving a sigh of relief as I drove away. Jackson slept on the back seat, oblivious to the dramas playing out in my head. It wasn't fair. Why couldn't nasty men look nasty, instead of, let's be honest, damned tasty. Sometimes life sucked.

At the Netherby house I made myself a hazelnut–flavoured coffee, helped myself to some biscuits that hadn't passed their use-by date, shared one with Jackson, then psyched myself up to tackle the shed. With an effort I managed to drag the heavy garage door open to reveal the gleaming vintage car. I thought of some of the magnificent hats I had seen in Maggie Netherby's wardrobe and it wasn't hard to imagine her driving the spectacular machine, looking like someone from an old movie. I was so tied up in my imagination, I jumped when I heard a car pull up outside. I ran out of the shed to see Senior Sergeant Carlton, in full police uniform but with the navy blue regulation trousers tucked securely into gumboots, coming towards me. He nodded towards the vintage car.

"Beauty, isn't she? It's probably worth more than the house."

'Yes it is a beauty. I certainly didn't expect to find anything so spectacular tucked in this old shed. Maggie Netherby had good taste."

"In some things. Never could see what she saw in old Gunna though"

"Maybe he has hidden talents," I laughed. "Still, it's a pity Gunna isn't here to tell me more about it. From what I am hearing he knew Maggie quite well. But I guess if he doesn't turn up, I'll just organise a tow-truck to take it to a sale yard."

"There's his caravan too," Carlton said. "That's why I'm here. I want to go down and search it to see if there's any sign of Gunna down there."

"Oh okay. Where's his caravan?" I asked.

Carlton pointed over the paddock to the shape I had assumed was an old shed.

"Down there. That roof. It's on Netherby land so I need to get your permission to search it. Are you okay with that?"

'Yeah. Fine by me. Can I come with you? I may as well see what's down there."

Carlton nodded and led the way over the paddock. I soon realised why he was wearing the stout gumboots. As my socks started to get wet inside my budget sneakers, I wished I had some too. Carlton must have read my thoughts as he put out a hand to stop me as we approached the lake edge.

"Be careful. It's pretty swampy around here."

I extricated a soggy sneaker from what had looked like

solid ground and nodded.

"Yep, I noticed."

I tip-toed and Carlton stomped through the edges of the swamp towards a patch of solid ground on which stood a dilapidated caravan that had once been yellow and white but was now rusty with a light coating of pale green slime. Surely nobody lived in it? Carlton pulled on the door handle but nothing happened.

"Is it locked?" I asked.

"I doubt it. Just old." Carlton yanked again and the door yielded. He grabbed the edge with both hands and pulled harder, the action making his shoulder muscles ripple under his police jacket. I stood back and admired the action until, with an ominous creak, the door opened enough to get through. I let Carlton do the honours, I had no desire to go inside. He didn't stay long either. I guess there weren't too many places to search as, almost immediately, he exited, shoving the door back into its slot.

"Well Gunna's certainly not in there, dead or alive," he said. "It's hard to tell when he was last here though. There's no leftover food, no dirty dishes, and even though this van looks like a dump outside, it's tidy inside."

"No handy diary with mysterious names in it?" I asked.

"No. A couple of dates circled on a generic calendar of duck pictures, but no secret messages," Carlton laughed. "Let's get back to dry ground."

As we made our way back up the paddock I pointed to an old woolshed tucked under some pine trees at what I assumed was the property's boundary.

"What about in there?" I asked. "Is it worth checking it out."

"I've already done that," Carlton answered. "I check that place regularly."

"Why?" I couldn't think of any reason why the local police would keep a check on a dilapidated woolshed.

"Because it's mine." The hard lines of Carlton's face softened in a smile as he enjoyed my surprise.

"Yours? Isn't it on Maggie Netherby's land? Aren't those pine trees the boundary?"

"No. The boundary is the fence line in front of it."

"And that property is yours? Your Maggie Netherby's neighbour?"

"Yep. Sort of. I don't live there. It's just open paddocks, no house. Just that shed and I'm not planning on living in that, although I do keep a few bits and pieces in it, which is why I check up on it. Stealing stuff from a cop always gets the local roughs a few extra bonus points. I bought the land as an investment and I rent out the grazing to a friend of mine who runs a few racehorses. Anyway, I'd better keep going. I've got a few other places to check this morning. We're pretty sure that Gunna must be dead, but in case he is lying somewhere injured, we have to look everywhere. Here," he rummaged in his pocket and pulled out a business card which he handed to me. "If you see anybody hanging around, give me a call, any time."

I agreed, then just as we reached his car, I threw him a question out of left field.

"What's up with you and Bruno McTavish? You both bad-mouth each other. What's your story?"

"Huh!" Carlton spat. "McTavish! He's nothing but trouble. Oh sure, he comes over all innocent and Mister Nice Guy but I've known him since primary school and I'm not fooled by all his Southern Man Hero shit. He needs to mind his own business and stop thinking that he's the Big Man. I'm watching him and the day he makes a mistake, I will be there to nail him."

The force of his anger surprised me so much I just nodded an "okay" as he threw himself into the police car, slammed his seatbelt on and revved the engine. As he drove away I realised I had missed the perfect opportunity to mention the gunshots in the night and the dead swans in Bruno's Land Rover. He had given me an opening and I hadn't taken it. Why was that?

I was still wondering that, and mentally comparing the good and bad attributes of the Southern Man and the Rugby Player, as I forced myself back into my work. I wrote myself a note to get the car moved into safe storage, then braced myself to go back into the shed and see what was in the back part.

It was worse than I imagined. I had psyched myself up to expect dust, spiders and old farm equipment that I didn't want to touch. If it had been like that, it wouldn't have revolted me as much. But it was clean. Incredibly clean. Scrubbed down, disinfected, scrupulously clean. Like a laboratory. Frankenstein's laboratory. I stood soundlessly, my hands clasped over my gaping mouth, as I took in the long work table, the knives, scalpels and other strangely shaped tools laid out at one end, the jars full of unidentifiable lumps and oddly coloured liquids at the other end, then the back wall where row upon row of stuffed swans, mallards, scaups and other birds perched on homemade shelves. Maggie Netherby was a taxidermist?

Transfixed, hands still covering my mouth, I slowly

approached the dead birds. Surely I wouldn't have to touch them? Surely I could just count them, and the weird tools and jars, then shut the door and never look at them again. Dead birds gave me the creeps and stuffed birds were worse. I always hated the bird room in the museum. While my parents wandered through it, pointing and discussing, I would pull my jersey over my head and run through as fast as I could. This wasn't any better.

Then I noticed the tags. Each bird had a label tied with string to its leg. I forced myself to get close enough to read one but it made no sense. The series of numbers, dashes and backslashes was obviously some form of code. I guessed it made sense to Maggie Netherby and was probably her way of keeping track of her taxidermy work, so I assumed that I would find some files somewhere to match the tags, but a look around the pristine workplace showed no sign of any filing system. It must be somewhere in the house. Or, I thought suddenly, maybe it wasn't Maggie's work. Maybe Gunna was the bird preserver; maybe the records were down in his caravan. But I wasn't going back down there today. I needed to buy myself some gumboots first. Plus, stuffed birds were low on my priority list. I had plenty of household goods to finish cataloguing first, and I still hadn't taken a good look at the hoard of boxes in the secret rooms. The birds could wait.

I looked at my watch but it wasn't telling me a time that I could justify as a meal break. I looked back up at the rows of birds and sighed. Okay, I was procrastinating and putting off stuff I didn't want to do. Really, there weren't that many birds and I needed to pull myself together. Putting things off was my worst habit. How long had I put off leaving Simon?

Far too long. This was the same thing on a much smaller scale. I needed to face the awful stuff and deal with it. If I knuckled down and started now, I could have the whole shed catalogued before lunch.

I had almost completed it and only had a few scaups left to enter onto my list when my phone rang. I glanced at the caller ID and my guess was right. Simon. I ignored it, letting it go to the answer machine, as the glowing numbers that showed the time suggested the reason for his call. I pictured him standing in the airport arrival lounge, feet apart, back straight, tie perfect, his face red with anger as the last passengers disembarked from the plane and I wasn't one of them. I knew that he wouldn't be yelling down the phone, he would be quietly seething, telling me in cold, clipped tones how I had failed him yet again, how inferior I was and what punishment I would receive to teach me how to improve myself. I set my phone to silent and turned back to the scaups.

Chapter 5

By the time I shut the door on the fully-documented shed, I felt smugly satisfied with myself. I had not only overcome my procrastination, I had actually achieved a lot. Sure, a lot of the notations read "bottle, unidentified contents, value tba (to be ascertained)" but there were several pages of notes. I deserved a lunch break.

Jackson thought I had forgotten him. He bounded off the couch, slid past me out the door and raced to the nearest tree. Well, at least he was housetrained. I called him back and was pleasantly surprised when he obeyed me, trotting back up the stairs and in the door. I gave him a pat then filled his food bowl with the tiny dog biscuits I was discovering were his favourite food, before raiding Maggie's pantry, settling for rather tasteless instant noodles washed down with more hazelnut coffee. To amuse myself I played back the rant Simon had left on my phone. It was exactly as I had expected, full of seething, angry, dominating threats. I nearly deleted it, then changed my mind. It was so nasty I decided to keep it to replay later to my friends and family and anyone else who thought he was wonderful and who was questioning my sanity in leaving him. They had only ever met Simon the perfectly hospitable successful businessman. This would show them the Simon I had lived with behind closed doors.

Closed doors. That was the next thing I had to gird my loins and deal with. The secret rooms and the hoard. It couldn't be any more disgusting than the stuffed birds –

unless it was more stuffed birds, crammed into mouldy boxes. Trying not to imagine the worst, I swung the bookcase door open and stepped through. It still smelt mouldy. The first room was practically empty apart from a pale blue Fender electric guitar resting against a cane chair in one corner. I wondered who had last played it. Through the next door, the hoard began. The boxes were stacked almost to the ceiling, with narrow pathways creating a twisting maze through the piles. I started with the box closest to me.

It was full of books. So were the next four boxes. I squeezed through the maze, opening other boxes at random. They were all the same. I went back to the first box, dragged it back to the empty room and tipped its contents out onto the floor. Paperbacks. Not academic texts or collectable books that would add some value to her estate, just pulp paperbacks. I found romances, westerns, science fiction, even children's books, some reasonably new and some aged, with yellowed pages and torn covers. I stuffed them back into the box, shoved it aside and moved to the next room. The same thing. Boxes of cheap books, even boxes of old magazines, although this time I noticed that many of the books were stamped with the names of second-hand book shops. Lots of different book shops. I began to wonder if Maggie Netherby had been a bit unhinged and had spent her time wandering through Dunedin bookshops buying cartons of books at a time, then storing them away like a pack rat. Had she ever read any of them? Or was she a prolific reader with eclectic tastes?

Not that the answer mattered. It didn't alter the fact that there were hundreds of boxes in each room and each box held at least twenty books, and I would have to check each one in case, amongst the trashy pulp fiction, there were any that were valuable. Dispirited, I pulled out my phone to call my boss. She answered promptly and I filled her in on the discovery of the hoard. I didn't mention Jackson, I would leave that revelation till later. Her response wasn't quite what I wanted. I had hoped that she would tell me to take as much time as I needed, but she did the opposite, reminding me of my next job and telling me to wind this one up as fast as possible. I hung up with the realisation that I would need to work well into the night for the next few days if I was to make her suggested deadline.

I needed a plan of action. I decided to find somewhere outside to dump each box if there was nothing good in it. I would start making a pile then I could ask Tom if he would help me take the worthless ones to the dump. I picked up the first box that I had already checked and carried it through to the lounge but, as I juggled the weight of the box on my hip and struggled with the front door, Jackson bolted through the gap. Cursing, I dumped the box and ran after him but by the time I had reached the bottom of the stairs, he was halfway across the paddock, heading for Gunna's caravan.

"Jackson, come back!" I screamed as I chased him, but he wasn't listening. I jumped the fence and hurried after him, calling his name frantically as I ran. When the ground started to feel squishy under my feet, and my light, still damp, shoes began to fill with water, his name got a few curse words added to it and by the time I caught up to him, standing hopefully outside the caravan door, I was ready to let off a Simon-style tirade about his manners and his pedigree. Jackson looked at me with his huge eyes and wagged his tail.

"Oh you..." I flopped down onto the caravan's small step. Jackson's tongue lolled as he panted, making him look as if he was smiling at me and laughing. "You rotten dog. Now my shoes are soaking. Still," I stood up and pulled on the caravan door, "while we're here, let's see if there's anything in here that gives me a clue about those tags on the dead birds in the shed."

It took all my strength to pull the door open, then Jackson pushed past me to get inside first. I followed to find him sniffing the air, and I had to agree it smelt like someone had been eating food in there recently. I wondered if it had smelt like that when Carlton was in here a few hours earlier, or had someone been here since then. As Carlton had said, the caravan was very tidy, with no signs that anyone had been in it, but it didn't feel empty. The bed was neatly made, covers pulled up with a straight edge on the top sheet as it folded down over the duvet, and on the shelf above the gas cooker, a plate, a mug and a breakfast bowl were perfectly lined up. There was something about the neatness that made me think of the pristine state of the laboratory-shed. Maybe Gunna was the taxidermist. He was obviously a neat-freak.

I felt guilty but that didn't stop me poking around, opening all the tiny cupboards, although I didn't see anything of interest until I gave up, grabbed Jackson by the collar and turned to leave. Above the door, tucked into the door frame, was a photograph; a candid snapshot of three people, all dressed in Swanndri jackets and hiking boots, all carrying shotguns and posing with an array of dead rabbits. I assumed that the woman was Maggie Netherby. I wasn't sure about the older man with the long, grey hair and straggly beard, although I guessed he could be the mysterious Gunna, but I definitely recognised the young man in the middle. Bruno McTavish.

Holding Jackson firmly by his collar, I manoeuvred him out of the caravan and back across the swampy ground. When we reached the firm grass of the paddock, I let him go, hoping he wouldn't run away again. I was wrong. He raced away like a rocket, his thin body curving and stretching as flew over the ground. At least he was heading in the right direction. I followed at a much slower pace, cursing my soggy sneakers with each squelching step. By the time I climbed over the fence, Jackson was already on the deck, bouncing with excitement at the Swanndri-clad figure leaning casually against the doorpost.

As I climbed the steps Bruno straightened up, flicking the errant lock of hair back from his stunning blue eyes. I blew out a long breath as I reached the top step, hoping that he thought I was just puffed and not realise I was trying to calm the feelings that erupted at the sight of him. Damn the man.

"Hi," he drawled, reaching down to scratch Jackson behind his ears. "You've got Jackson."

"Um, obviously."

"Yeah, that was a pretty stupid statement, wasn't it. I mean, I didn't know you had collected him. I thought he was still in the pound. But I am so glad you've got him. Are you going to keep him? Or are you going to give him to the Atkins boys?"

"The Atkins boys? Oh, is that the J brothers? I don't think so. The pound lady talked me into taking him. Well, Jackson's big eyes helped win me over. But she was adamant that he not go to them because he isn't a hunting dog and wouldn't survive in a kennel."

"She was right, not in our winter at his age, he won't. So what are you going to do with him? I've been trying to find someone suitable, so I can keep asking around if you like."

"No, that won't be necessary. I have no idea how I am going to work it out, but even if it means getting a new apartment in Wellington, I'm going to keep him. Unless he runs away from me again, in which case he's...," I glared at Jackson with my best angry face but he wagged his tail to show he knew I was joking, "going...to...be...my dinner."

Bruno didn't believe me any more than Jackson did. He laughed.

"Yeah, right. Anyway, I saw you coming up from Gunna's van. Did you go inside? Is he there? Is there any sign of him?"

"Yes, no, no," I answered all his questions at once. "Yes, I went in but no, it doesn't look as if anyone's been there." I didn't mention the smell of food as it could have been nothing. Maybe the caravan always smelt that way.

"Damn! I'm really starting to think that arm must be his. I keep hoping that he'll turn up at the pub and say it's all a prank, but that's getting less and less likely."

"Do you know him well? I saw a photo down there with you in it. I presume the others were Maggie Netherby and Gunna."

"Yeah, The annual rabbit drive over in Cromwell. Maggie cleaned up that year. She was a damned good shot." He paused, a question forming in his mind. "Are her guns still locked up safely? And is Gunna's one with them?"

I shook my head. "I haven't seen any guns. Where would they be?"

"In the gun cabinet." He made it sound as if I was the

village idiot for having to ask.

"What gun cabinet?" I asked, trying to match his belittling tone with some attitude of my own. "So far, I haven't found one."

"Really?" Bruno's brow furrowed in confusion. "It's in one of the back rooms. Knowing Maggie, it's probably got something ordinary hanging in front of it so it doesn't look obvious. She was pretty tight on gun safety."

"I will add it to my list of things to sort through," I said.

"Okay, let me know if you find it." Bruno checked his watch. "I'd better be going. I only stopped by to see if I could check out the caravan, but if you've done that and Gunna isn't there, I'll keep going."

"Okay. Senior Sergeant Carlton checked out the caravan earlier today. He's looking everywhere for Gunna too."

"I'll bet he isn't," Bruno spat. "He'll look like he's looking but I bet he's hoping to find him dead."

"Wow! That's nasty. He looked and sounded like a policeman doing his job. He's checking everywhere in case Gunna's lying somewhere injured. Are you doing that?"

Bruno drew himself to his full height to fend off my insult, his eyes flashing as he stepped forwards, making me step aside to let him past.

"Yes. Yes I bloody well am. And, unlike that weasel, I actually care."

As he stormed off, I grabbed Jackson by the collar to stop him following. Without waiting to see Bruno drive away, I pushed the dog through the door and locked it behind us. If Carlton was a weasel, that infuriatingly good looking hunk was a stoat, or some other equally horrid, sleazy, low-life creature.

Damn him and damn the fact that my feet were wet and freezing cold. Muttering an apology to Maggie under my breath, I pulled off my sodden sneakers and socks and padded barefoot through to her bedroom where I rifled through the drawers, borrowing a pair of heavy wool socks and a pair of purple, fluffy slippers that sat in her wardrobe alongside several pairs of stout lace-up leather shoes and a well-worn pair of hiking boots. They were too large but I didn't care as they were warm and comfortable.

Then I remembered the box of books that had started the earlier drama. It was still on the deck where I had dropped it in my haste to catch Jackson. I stared at it through the glass door. It could stay there for now, I would go to Plan B and instead of taking them out one at a time as I finished with them, I would stack the checked boxes in the first secret room, which meant I could do my favourite thing and procrastinate. I could put off thinking about getting them outside until I had no other option left.

I worked steadily through the boxes, widening the pathway through the maze and I had almost cleared a path through to the boarded-up window in the far wall when the encroaching darkness stopped me seeing what I was doing. What little light that had been filtering through the small gaps between the boards had dimmed to almost nothing and I was struggling to read the book titles. I stood up, my back cracking as I stretched to relieve the ache in my muscles.

The room that had contained just a guitar and a chair was now full with boxes stacked as high as I could easily lift them. Maggie's stacks were two, sometimes three, boxes higher so she must have been a strong woman. With a satisfied look back at what I had achieved, I stepped through to the lounge and pushed the secret door shut. The lounge was dark but I wasn't planning on staying any longer, so there was no reason to turn on the lights. Instead, I fumbled in the gloom for my sneakers, grimacing as the dampness penetrated Maggie's thick socks.

"Okay, Jackson," I called to the blanket mound on the couch, "let's go."

Jackson walked placidly beside me out the door and all the way to my car before he bolted. Just as I reached forwards to open the door, he was gone, crossing the fence in a fluid leap and racing across the paddock. I sighed. Another soggy trip to the caravan and, this time, in the dark. Why had I not clipped his lead to his collar? I had a lot to learn about owning a whippet. I didn't bother wasting my breath calling his name, I had already figured out that he went deaf when he was running. I hunted around in the depths of my bag and found my torch, cursing its pathetically small beam. Still, it was better than nothing. Marginally.

I gave up on the torch before I climbed the fence, shoving it into my jacket pocket when I needed both hands to hold onto the post and the wire as I swayed and floundered my way over. If this was the fastest way to get from the house to Gunna's caravan why had they never built a gate? Or even an old-fashioned stile? In the paddock I stopped to get my bearings, hoping my night vision would improve before I got to the tricky part. I peered towards the caravan, trying to make out a doggy shape in the gloom. Then I saw him. Again, it was too late to call out as he was running, but not towards me. Chasing something only he could see, Jackson raced sideways across the paddock towards the boundary and the woolshed that I had thought was Maggie's, forcing me to change my direction and trudge after him, praying that there were no hidden rabbit holes to fall into, then praying that it wasn't rabbits Jackson was chasing and that he wouldn't follow them underground and get stuck. At least my night vision was getting better and I could almost make out what I was tripping over as I stumbled along, puffing and swearing.

The woolshed was built into the slope of the hill so it was two-storeyed on the downhill side I was approaching from. I peered through a large gap in the rusting tin cladding, hoping it was Jackson I could hear inside and not a pack of large, hungry rats. Whatever it was suddenly moved and snorted. I pulled back in panic. Pressing my back against the outside of the woolshed, hoping the thing inside wouldn't see or smell me, I sat, shaking, forcing myself to breathe. Whatever it was, it wasn't Jackson and it was way too big to be a rat. It snorted again. I didn't want to know what it was but I had to know. Not knowing was much more terrifying than anything it could possibly be. I knew Otago seemed like a step back in time from Wellington, but it wasn't Jurassic so I wrote off T-Rex as a possibility and started to think logically. The beast grunted. I plucked up all my courage, sucked in a deep breath, pulled out my pathetic torch, flicked it on and shone the beam through the gap in the wall.

In the beam the beast's eyes glowed red. All four of them. I clapped my hand to my mouth to choke back the scream, muttering "oh my god, oh my god, oh my god" as I sank back against the wall. Four eyes. It has four eyes! What monster has four eyes? Then I almost giggled. Two monsters. Two monsters with two eyes each. I looked again and was almost relieved to make out their huge bodies. At least they were something I recognised. Pigs. More bloody pigs! Huge pigs, even bigger than the one I had seen on Bruno's Land Rover. I shuddered at the sight of the tusks protruding well past their noses.

"I wouldn't want to meet them in the dark," I whispered to myself, then smiled as I realised that I had actually done just that. However, that didn't solve my problem, it just made it more difficult. I still hadn't found Jackson and now I would have to get past the pigs to get inside. Unless there was another way in.

I stuffed my torch back in my pocket, relying on feel to make my way around the edge of the building, searching for a door. On the tallest side of the building I found myself under the ramps that would have taken the sheep back into the paddock after they had been shorn in the main floor of the shed. There was a small doorway under the ramps and it was open as the door had long ago fallen off its hinges and rotted on the ground. I stepped over its remains, ducking my head to get through the tiny gap. The smell was intense.

As a Wellington office worker, my only dealings with pigs were ham sandwiches and rashers of bacon. I had heard stories of pigs being dirty but I wasn't prepared for the smell that hit me. More than just dirt, this was decay. Once in the early days of my career, I had been given the task of valuing a property where an old man had died, then lain for several weeks before he was found. Although his house had been cleaned, the smell of his decomposing body had still been present, tainting the walls, and this was the same. There may have been two live pigs under the woolshed, but there was something else under there, something well past dead. I needed to find Jackson and get out of there.

Above me, on the main floor, the floorboards creaked. Could Jackson be up there? I was about to back out the door when the floorboards creaked again with the distinctive sounds of human footsteps. I froze. Someone was up there. Then a voice spoke and I realised that, like the pigs, there were two of them. I could tell from the depth of the voices that they were male, but I couldn't make out what they were saying, or what they were doing. The footsteps went backwards and forwards above my head, then there was a loud thump as if they had dropped something heavy, followed by scraping as they dragged whatever it was across the floor. I squeezed myself into a tight ball against the wall, barely daring to breathe in case they heard me.

Who were they? What were they doing in Carlton's woolshed? Could it be Gunna? Could the dragging be someone injured, desperately trying to pull themselves to safety? Should I go and check? I rejected that idea quickly. Carlton had already checked the woolshed for Gunna. If he was up there, injured, he would have been found already. So, who else would it be? Hadn't Carlton told me people liked to steal stuff from him? Maybe I should tell him. Fumbling in the dark, I pulled out my phone and, with a bit of searching through my pockets, found the rumpled business card Carlton had given me. I used the light on my phone to squint at the card, then thumbed in the number and hit dial.

Above me a phone rang. Startled, I cancelled my call, then felt foolish. It must be Carlton upstairs, in his own woolshed, doing whatever he was entitled to do in his own place, even if it was at night, in the dark. If he had answered, I could have just admitted that I was down with the pigs, looking for Jackson, but I couldn't ring back. I would feel too stupid trying to explain why I had hung up. I sat back on the damp floor, hoping he would think it was a wrong number and ignore it.

I heard him say something, then I felt my own phone vibrate. I refused the call as quickly as I could, feeling absurdly grateful to Simon that his annoying persistence had forced me to keep my phone on silent mode. Later Carlton might work out that it was me who called, but by then I could pretend I had been at the Netherby house, not crouching in his pigsty. Even if I hadn't found Jackson, it was time to leave.

As I tensed my muscles to stand up, somewhere in front of me, in the dark, the pigs grunted. Above me another grunt seemed to reply, then the roof creaked and a chink of light shone through a gap. More grunting and creaking turned the gap into a trapdoor through which a man's head appeared, his face shadowed into anonymity. Near me the pigs squealed.

"They okay?" I recognised the voice as Carlton.

"Yep," the face in the trapdoor replied.

"Okay, chuck it in," Carlton ordered as the man pulled back from the hole.

I stepped back as far as I could as a torrent of vegetable scraps poured through the trapdoor. Then the man was back in the hole, sweeping a strong torch beam across the pigs. I was happy that it showed strong wire mesh gates between the pigs and my hiding place. At least they couldn't reach me.

"What about the dog?" I heard the man ask.

"Yeah," Carlton replied. "Chuck it in too."

I almost screamed. Jackson? They had Jackson and they were going to throw him to the pigs? Then, before I could move, a carcass dropped through the roof. I held my breath, trying not to vomit as it plunged downward, then stifled my tears of relief as I realised it was too big to be Jackson. Some poor hunting dog. I turned away, blocking my ears from the sound of the pigs tearing the dead dog apart, fighting to stop the rising panic. I needed to keep calm and get out. Fast.

Moving as silently as I could, I crept back through the tiny door and around the side of the building, then I hunkered down in the shadows to think. What if they saw me going back across the paddock? I made a plan. If I walked around to the front of the shed and approached boldly, they would think I had just arrived and I could tell them I was looking for Jackson, ask if they had seen him, rattle off some inane pleasantries and leave. It wasn't the greatest plan but it was the only one I could think of. Then two things happened at once.

I was still sitting in the shadows when Jackson appeared, racing across the paddock back towards his home. At the same time, the man who wasn't Carlton walked around the side of the building, lifting a rifle to his shoulder.

"Look," he called to Carlton. "There he is. I'll get the bastard this time."

"Leave it alone," Carlton called back. "Don't waste your ammo, it's only a bloody whippet. It's not a threat. It can't talk."

"Don't care. I hate that bloody dog."

I willed Jackson to keep running, a few more metres and he would be through the fence and safely on Maggie's porch, but he stopped at just the wrong moment. As Jackson's head turned back towards me, the man sighted down the barrel and pulled the trigger. Jackson's scream told me the shot was accurate. Behind me I heard Carlton pull the other man away, then their car engine revved and they sped off down the road. I didn't care if they looked back and saw me. I ran as fast as I could, stumbling over rabbit holes, sobbing with grief, towards the limp figure who had nearly made it to the safety of our boundary fence.

He was still alive. The bullet had pierced his thigh but he was conscious, whimpering as I approached. I had no idea what to do, but I had done a human first aid course once so I figured the principles were the same. I pulled off Maggie's damp socks, used one of them as padding for the wound, then tied it on with the other sock. Carefully, scared that I would hurt him more but desperate to get him somewhere safe, I wrapped Jackson in my jacket, picked him up and carried him, struggling over the rough ground. He was heavier than I expected. In the dark the few metres to the fence seemed to take forever but then I was there, sliding him underneath the fence before climbing over to carry him to my car.

I needed to find a vet urgently. Gail would know. I started to phone her then remembered a sign I had seen near the pound in Mosgiel. There was a vet clinic there that said 24 hours. Spraying gravel from the tyres, I drove fast, urging Jackson to stay alive as I threw the car around the twisting country roads, and sped down the highway through the darkness of the Taieri Plains. When I reached the township, I struggled to remember directions that had been easy to find in the daylight, but after a couple of wrong turns, I found the pound, then the vet clinic a few doors away. The sign said 24 hours, but it was dark and closed.

Frustrated, almost crying, I got out of the car to check,

only to find a bell and a large notice telling me to push the bell for emergencies. I pushed. When no lights came on I pushed again, for longer. Surely someone was there. As I was about to try a third time, the porch lit up and the door opened. I gasped in amazement. Standing in striped pyjama pants, pulling a white coat over the rippling muscles of his bare chest, running his hands through his sleep-tousled hair, was Bruno McTavish.

"You're the vet?" I gasped.

"What's wrong?" he asked, ignoring my question.

"It's Jackson. He's been shot."

Bruno rushed past me, lifting Jackson gently from the car to carry him inside. I followed him through to an examination room where he lay Jackson on the stainless steel bench and removed my jacket and temporary sock dressing.

"Good work on the first aid," he said as he probed the wound. "What happened? Here, keep Jackson still while you're talking, I need to get him anaesthetised so I can take out the bullet."

I followed Bruno's orders, trying to be helpful as he removed the bullet that was still embedded in Jackson's thigh muscle, and while he worked, I told him everything, about the shooting and about the pigs.

"It wasn't Carlton who shot Jackson," I finished. "It was the other guy, but I don't know who he was."

"I've got a pretty fair idea," Bruno growled as he closed the cleaned wound with a neat row of stitches. "I'll get the bastard. He's not getting away with this. Now, let's put Jackson in a warm cage to sleep this off and we'll get a coffee. Looks like you need one as much as I do."

Bruno escorted me to his living quarters at the back of the clinic where he discarded his coat into a laundry hamper, forcing me to stare at his tight abs as he made us coffee, which he served with a packet of chocolate biscuits.

"For strength in emergencies," he explained as he pushed the packet towards me.

I took two, munching them as I settled into his oversized leather couch, trying hard to distract myself from the nearness of his semi-naked body. He seemed completely unaware of my distress.

"Run the whole thing by me again," he said. "I didn't take it all in before, my mind was on Jackson."

When I had finished, Bruno sat forward, letting out his breath in a long whistle while he pummelled the fist of one hand into the palm of the other.

"Wow! You must have been terrified." He looked at me and smiled. "But you might have just given me the nail to finally close Carlton's coffin. I knew it was him. I've been so sure of that for ages, but I've never been able to prove it. Now, thanks to you, I think I can. If I act fast."

"Prove what? Apart from shooting Jackson, which was the other guy, Carlton hasn't done anything, has he? It's not illegal to have smelly pigs, is it? Is it even illegal to feed them dead dogs?"

"No, you're right, that might be gross but I don't think it's illegal either, unless he stole the dog. No, keeping the pigs isn't the illegal bit. It's where he got them from and what they are doing with them that's going to get him in trouble. But," Bruno stood up, reached out his hand to take mine and drew me up from the couch, "enough for now. It's a long story and it's late. Way too late for you to be driving home.

So, my bedroom's through that door. Take my bed and get some sleep while I go and check on Jackson. We can talk more in the morning."

"I can't take your bed," I protested. "Just give me a blanket and I will be quite comfy here on the couch."

"I insist."

"And you lose." I pulled my hand away from his and sat back on the couch. "Stop fussing. I am just glad Jackson is going to be okay. So get me a blanket then go and do your vet thing. And thank you. I have never been so scared. All the way here I thought Jackson was going to die. I've only had him for a couple of days and already I don't know how what I would do if anything happened to him."

"Okay, you win. Come with me. Let's go and see how he's doing."

Together we walked back to the clinic where we found Jackson sleeping peacefully in spite of the intravenous drip silently pumping fluid into his veins. Satisfied, we returned to Bruno's lounge, where he opened a cupboard, handed me a blanket and a pillow and smiled in defeat.

"Good night, Andrea North. Try and get some sleep because tomorrow, we are going to take down the devil."

Chapter 6

I woke to my favourite kind of pig. Bacon and abs. I wasn't sure what was more enticing – the smell of coffee and sizzling bacon, or the sight of Bruno, still shirtless, striped pyjama pants replaced by faded blue jeans sitting snug against his hips. For a few moments, I pretended to be still asleep so I could watch him, then I felt guilty and was sure he knew what I was doing, so I made a big show of yawning and stretching and tried to sound nonchalant as I said good morning. He smiled back, held up the electric jug and raised his eyes in a question.

"Tea or coffee?"

"Coffee please," I said, pulling myself up from the couch, "Black, no sugar."

"Something else we have in common," Bruno quipped as he poured two cups.

"Something else? Other than what? Do we have anything in common?"

"Of course we do. Jackson for starters. He's looking good this morning, by the way. I checked on him earlier and he's doing well. He was just damned lucky that the bullet got his thigh where he has a lot of muscle. It's going to leave a permanent scar and he will be limping for a while, but I'm pretty sure he's going to pull through this just fine. Hope you like bacon."

"After last night you'd think it would be the last thing I wanted to eat but that does smell really good, so, yes thanks, bacon would be awesome."

Bruno served the perfectly cooked bacon and eggs on surprisingly dainty plates edged in pastel blue flowers, at a table so small our knees touched each other as we sat. I wasn't sure if I felt embarrassed or excited every time we accidentally made contact and, by the slight flush in his cheeks, I wondered if he was feeling the same way, especially when he found an excuse to walk to the bench, then purposefully sat sideways when he returned. The bacon was exquisite, so I told him so.

"Glad you like it," he replied with a grin. "I wasn't sure if you were a big fan of home-kill and after I started cooking it I had a sudden fear that you might even be vegetarian."

"What made you think that?"

"I don't know," he shrugged, shamefaced. "You know, you're a Wellington city girl, not one of us country bumpkins, and we didn't get off to a very good start. You didn't seem too fond of pigs that day."

"That day, I didn't have any problems at all with the pig. It was your dreadful driving, if you remember."

"Yeah, well, I did have a good reason for driving so fast. It was an emergency. I bet you weren't doing 30k yourself around those bends last night."

'True," I admitted, "but I thought Jackson was dying and that pig looked like it was already dead."

"And it was. But one of my clients in the village had rung me all agitated. Her little dog was having puppies and one was stuck. So I was in a rush to get there. I, too, thought a dog was dying."

"But by the time I got there, you were at the pub, drinking."

"Yes I was. Fortunately, by the time I got to my client's

house, the dog had delivered the pup naturally and the panic was over. I checked them all, gave the owner some reassurance, then stopped at the pub to organise the pig. By the way, the bacon you're eating is from the same source. Pretty tasty, eh?"

I was glad he said that with a laugh but I still got the distinct impression that I should shut up while I was winning. Anyway, I felt pretty stupid. I had misjudged him badly, something I was too good at doing when it came to men. I had misjudged Simon, mistaking arrogance and domination for confidence, I might have misjudged Carlton, and I had certainly misjudged Bruno. My track record was abysmal. Maybe I should stick to whippets.

I was just about to find a conversation topic that wouldn't get me in trouble when, at the front of the building, a door slammed and a cheery voice called out to Bruno.

"Hi," he called back. "Out the back."

His response froze my heart. Was this Amy? I had forgotten about her. The girlfriend who was going to be angry with him for not getting home on time. Damn Amy. I started to think of ways to leave politely but quickly. How would she react to seeing me here, eating breakfast with her boyfriend? Especially as he had no shirt on and I didn't think I looked as if I was there on business. What would I say to her? Then she bounced into the room and I stared in shock. She was stunning; tall, athletic, with long, dark hair pulled back in a high pony tail on the top of her head but it was her clothes that made the impact. Over practical jeans and t-shirt she wore a white lab coat, a name tag looking official on her breast.

"Joan, this is Andy North," Bruno introduced her. "Andy,

Joan Mexted, the other vet who works here. She keeps this place running while I'm driving pigs around country roads."

"Hi, Joan." I extended my hand, hoping I didn't look as foolish as I felt. Why had I automatically thought she was his girlfriend and so, somehow, my rival. Rival for what?

"Come and see Jackson," Bruno continued. "Andy brought him in last night. Some bastard shot him."

"What?" Joan's reaction was genuine anger. "Jackson the whippet? Really? Who would do that? Is he going to be all right?"

I followed them back to the clinic where Bruno handed Joan some paperwork and spoke to her in medical jargon. I knelt down in front of Jackson's cage so I could reach through the bars to pat him. He lifted his head in response, slowly wagging his tail at my touch.

"The answer to who would do that is our good friend Carlton, or at least one of his mates," Bruno said. "And, finally, I might have something I can pin on him. So I'm leaving Jackson in your tender care and I'm heading back up to the Netherby place with Andy. Text me if I'm needed anywhere urgently, but otherwise, the clinic's all yours. I'll be back but I can't guarantee when." He turned to me. "Okay, Andy, let's get a move on. I'll take my car and follow you."

"Um, you've forgotten something," Joan said tactfully, rolling her eyes as if it wasn't a new experience.

"What?" Bruno asked then laughed as Joan simply pointed to his bare chest. "Oh, yeah, sorry." I was more sorry when he came back, another plaid, woollen Swanndri covering his delectable abs.

I wanted to find out more about what he expected to find at the woolshed but, as we were driving in convoy, all I could do was concentrate on the road. Answers would have to wait until we got to the Netherby house so, instead, I created all sorts of scenarios in my head about getting there and finding Carlton waiting for me. In some scenarios he was friendly, happily accepting my excuse about the phone call, and in others he was shoulder to shoulder with his mate with the gun, demanding Jackson's body for his pigs. A country song came on the radio so I turned it up and sang along to drown out my own thoughts.

The Netherby house was just as I had left it. There were no police cars in the driveway and no men with guns. Just Bruno's Land Rover pulling in behind me. My eyes widened as he pulled a rifle from behind the seat but I didn't question him, just followed meekly as he led the way across the fence to the woolshed. I caught up to him as we approached, tapped him on the shoulder to get his attention and pointed out the door under the ramp. Bruno hoisted his rifle onto his shoulder by its leather strap, beckoning me to follow him though the doorway where I got my first decent look at the monster pigs.

With sunlight streaking through the many holes in the rotting shell of the woolshed, the full horror of the pigsty was revealed.

"What the hell?" Bruno gasped.

The ground floor of the woolshed was about half the size of the main floor above it. We could stand easily once we had ducked through the tiny doorway, but the hill it was built on was steep, so standing room rapidly disappeared as the ground rose to meet the ceiling. About two metres in front of us the heavy-duty mesh fence separated us from the pigs who, in daylight, proved to be even bigger than they had seemed in the dark. They were massive. In my head pigs were smooth, pink and kind of cute, but these guys were anything but cuddly. Their black, mottled skin was covered in rough hair which, in turn, was covered in brown, slimy, smelly mud.

"This is disgusting." Bruno whipped a handkerchief from his pocket and held it to his nose.

"Oh, yes." I agreed, doing the same. I stepped closer to the fence to get a better look at the huge animals who had moved away from us to the back of their pen. "Why are they here? I mean, okay, I get that Carlton can keep pigs in his own shed, but why are they down here in the dark instead of, I don't know, outside in a pen?"

"I'm going to let you answer your own question," Bruno said. I noticed that he didn't walk forwards to join me but stood well back. He obviously knew more about pigs than I did. "Why would you stash something away in a secret place?"

"Because I didn't want anyone to know I had it?" I replied, playing his game.

"And why would you not want people to know you had something?"

"Because I shouldn't have had it in the first place."

"Exactly."

"Oh, is this what you meant when you said that where he got them from was the illegal bit? Is your friendly local policeman a thief in his spare time?"

"Not quite. It's a bit more complicated than that. But let's look around and see what else my old buddy Ian has got stashed away down here. What smells so bad?"

"Isn't it just the pigs?"

"I don't think so. Sure, they smell pretty bad and I doubt that pen has ever been cleaned out, but there's something more. Can you smell it?"

"I'm trying not to, but I agree. I noticed it last night. There's something rotten down here."

"What's that over there?" Bruno passed the edge of the pig pen and headed into the gap between the fence and the sloping wall. I followed, catching up with him just as he reached forwards to lift the edge of a large, black tarpaulin that covered a waist-high mound of indeterminate shape. I didn't have time to see anything except a flash of white before Bruno dropped the tarpaulin and rushed past me, hand to his mouth. It didn't take a rocket scientist to work out that whatever was under the tarp was nasty and, by the smell, very dead.

Back outside, I found Bruno leaning against the sheep ramp, looking green around the gills.

"Bloody hell," he pushed his hair out of his eyes. "I'm a vet. You'd think I'd be used to stuff like that."

"Stuff like what? I saw something white that looked like feathers. Oh my god, surely not? Is that a pile of dead swans?"

"I don't know. Might be. Sorry, it threw me. Give me a few minutes to breathe some fresh air and I'll have another look. I'll be prepared for the worst this time."

Bruno paced for a few moments, obviously steeling himself for what he might find, then he blew out a long breath, flexed his shoulders and beckoned me to follow.

"You don't have to watch if you don't want to," he said as we reached the covered pile.

"Thanks. I'm not sure if I want to see it or not," I

admitted. "I'll just stand back here a bit for now. You're welcome to the yukky stuff."

"Gee, thanks. Right." He took hold of the edge of the tarp. "Here goes nothing. Three, two one."

We stared in silence.

"You utter bastard!" Bruno swore. "You utter, utter, absolute, scum-of-the-earth, piece-of-shit bastard!"

I didn't say anything. I was too transfixed by the sight of the pile to find any words. The white feathers I thought I had seen were mixed with black ones, thousands of them, but it was the eyes that held me speechless. Swan heads staring at us through sightless eyes, their graceful long necks elegant even in decay, piled at random, separated from their bodies which lay where they had been thrown.

"Look at that," Bruno said, pointing to a carcass. "Just the breast meat taken. What a bloody waste. I am so going to take him down now. Have you got your phone?"

"Yes. Why? Who am I calling?"

"Nobody. Just start taking pictures." He pulled out his own phone, thumbed the camera icon and started clicking madly. "You photograph the pigs and I'll do this lot."

I had taken about ten shots of the pigs and their enclosure when Bruno swore, stepped into the mess of decaying swans and started pulling the pile apart.

"No, no, no, no, no," he chanted as he tore into the birds. "Please, no."

He stopped suddenly and pointed his phone to click off more pictures, reaching forwards between each shot to expose more of the object of his horror. I stepped forwards to see what it was, but Bruno held out his hand to stop me.

"What is it?" I asked.

"It's not a what," Bruno replied. "It's a who. Or at least, another part of the who."

He held out his phone to me and I looked at the last picture he had taken. It was past individual recognition but it was still easily identifiable as a skull, and it was obviously not from a swan or a pig.

"Let's get the hell out of here," Bruno suggested.

In full agreement, I was ready to run as soon as we got out of the woolshed but Bruno reached out his hand to hold me back, forcing me to calm down and walk sedately across the paddock. When we reached the fence, he climbed over first, then held the wire down with one hand, offering me the other to steady myself as I climbed over. I swear my stumble that made me fall into his arms wasn't intentional but, for a split second, I forgot the horrors in the woolshed. As he steadied me, I felt the strength of his body through the comforting warmth of the woollen Swanndri mirrored by the depth of his sparkling blue eyes that flashed with amusement as I looked up to apologise.

"Woah," he laughed. "Steady on. You okay?"

"Yeah, sorry. Not good at this country stuff." I put the rush of blood to my face down to adrenalin, not a teenage blush. "You know, in the big city we have these amazing things called gates."

Bruno pretended to look confused. "Gates? What are they? Never heard of them." Then he flashed me another smile, let me go and turned towards his car, pulling the rifle from his shoulder as he walked, leaving me unsure if the moment had happened or not. For a second it had seemed like he had held me just a bit longer than was necessary, and just a bit tighter. Or had I imagined that? Was I reading far more into the situation than was there? "Get a grip," I told myself, under my breath in case he heard me, but my heart was still racing as I made my way up the steps to the house.

Back in the safety of Maggie Netherby's lounge, with the sun streaming through the windows and the waters of the lake glistening in the background, the gruesome pictures on our phones seemed unreal. To give us both a chance to let our brains settle and process what we had just seen, I made us a coffee, remembering that Bruno had his black like I did, and I tried not to notice how close he was as we sat side by side on the couch, staring at the small screen of his phone. One by one, Bruno scrolled through long shots of the whole pile to give reference, then close-ups of individual pieces of swans - heads, legs, bones - until he reached the last few pictures. He zoomed into a shot and I could clearly see what had started his frantic search through the pile of decay – tangled among the black and white feathers there was a flash of blue.

"What is that?" I grabbed his arm to pull the phone closer.

In reply, Bruno tugged at his clothes. "My guess is a swanny. Or a piece of one, anyway."

"A swan? They're all swans and swans aren't blue."

"Not a swan, a swanny. A Swanndri jacket, like this one," he tugged his jacket again, " only blue."

"Oh." I wasn't sure how to answer that.

"One good thing, though, sort of."

"What?"

"Gunna's swanny is green."

"Oh." I thought about that for a moment. "So if it isn't Gunna's jacket, then the rest of the bits might not be Gunna?

"Exactly. I don't know who this poor bastard is, but with a

bit of luck, it isn't Gunna."

"So where is he?"

"You know," Bruno pulled himself off the couch and strode to the window where he stared down at the lake, "I was going to say I didn't know, but maybe I do. If Gunna is hiding out, maybe I just might have an inkling where he could be. Do you fancy some cross-country walking? I hope you've got some gumboots."

"Damn, no I don't." I waggled a foot in the air. "I'm still wearing my ruined sneakers from yesterday, but my shoes are never going to be the same again, so I guess it doesn't matter if they get wet. Again. Let me guess, we're going back down to his caravan?"

"And a bit further." Bruno gave me an enigmatic smirk which did not fill me with any reassurance whatsoever. "Are you game for a yomp?"

"A what? That sounds disgusting."

"A yomp. Wonderful word, isn't it. I learnt it from Gunna. He yomps a lot." He flashed another of those heart-stopping smiles. "Long-distance trekking. Over rough terrain. In full military kit, but we can forget that bit, except I might take my rifle. You never know, it might come in handy."

I groaned. "Oh fabulous. That sounds just peachy. Okay, if we have to do it, let's get it over with." I stood up and waved an arm to acknowledge the door. "After you, yomp leader. lead the way."

We were halfway down the paddock before I remembered that Bruno had not explained the meaning of the pigs in the woolshed, or why them being there was illegal. I asked.

"You're right," Bruno answered without slowing his rapid pace across the field. "But not now. Let's see if I'm right about Gunna, then I promise to reveal all."

"Don't I wish," I thought to myself, conjuring up memories of this bare chest as I watched his lean body striding ahead of me.

Cross-country walking obviously came naturally to Bruno but it wasn't something I did regularly in inner-city Wellington, so I was panting and red-faced by the time I caught up with him at the swampy lake edge where I followed in his footsteps through the wet ground to the caravan. It looked exactly as I had last seen it, but I had a funny feeling that someone had been there. I could tell by the worried expression on Bruno's face that he thought the same. There was nothing positive to show that anyone was there, but it didn't feel empty. I let Bruno wrestle with the sticking door and enter first. Just as Jackson had, he sniffed the air.

"Someone's been in here. I can smell food."

"Jackson thought that yesterday," I said.

"Told you that, did he?" Bruno laughed.

"Yes, he did, actually. In whippet talk. Seriously, he sniffed around and I had to agree with him. I thought someone had been eating food in here too."

"Which means Gunna..."

"Must be around," I finished his sentence.

Bruno knelt down to feel a dark patch on the stained carpet. "And I am even more sure now that I know where he is. He's out there." He pointed out towards the lake.

"In the water? What, he's hiding in a boat?"

"No, not quite. Come on."

He shepherded me out of the caravan, pulled the door shut, checked the position of his rifle on his shoulder and led the way across the marshy ground, turning back to help me every time I lost my footing and squished into the oozing mud that gradually took over from the solid patches of green grass.

"Oh yuk!" I said for the hundredth time as I sank up to my ankles. "Where are we going?"

Bruno didn't answer. He kept walking, blithely picking the dry patches that seemed to disappear beneath me when I tried to follow. As we pushed forwards through a tall patch of reeds, a loud hissing noise stopped him in his tracks and I, head down to concentrate on the vanishing ground, crashed into him.

"Shhh," he whispered as caught my shoulders to steady me. "Keep quiet and walk back, slowly."

I tried to peer past Bruno to see what we were avoiding but couldn't see anything except tall, damp vegetation and, as his tight, determined grip pushed me backwards, I had no alternative but to do as he said. I shrugged myself free from his hands, turned and felt my way back through the marsh until I found a large dry patch. When I turned back I realised Bruno was doing the same thing, only backwards, his eyes fixed firmly on the piece of swamp we had just left.

"What's in there?" I whispered. "And why are we whispering?"

"A black swan's nest," Bruno replied in his normal voice, "and we don't have to whisper any more. I think we are far enough away for him not to bother us."

"Him? Who's him?"

"The male swan. I didn't see him but I heard him hiss. He will be out there not too far away and he will be very protective of his wife and her eggs. There is no way I am getting between him and them. An angry swan can be dangerous. They are a big, strong bird"

"Oh, okay." I strained my eyes but I still couldn't see either the nest or a swan. "So how do we get around them? I'm not swimming."

"Don't worry, neither am I. Let me think. We need to get..." Bruno pointed to a mound of grass a few metres away but past the edge of the last of the dry ground, "over there. I know it's possible to walk there if you know the right places to step, but it's been a while and, I now fully admit, that with the swan family in residence on the only track I know, I have no ideas left. A boat would be nice but I haven't got one."

"Why?"

"Because I didn't know I would need one."

"No, not why haven't you got a boat. Why do you want to go over there? Is that where you think Gunna is?" I peered at the mound of grass. "He can't be there, wouldn't we see him?"

"No, we wouldn't, that's the whole point. It's a mai-mai." He laughed at my blank stare of incomprehension. "A duck hunter's blind. It might look like tall grass but under that camouflage is a surprisingly spacious, well-appointed hut complete with chairs and a gas cooker. I have spent many cold but enjoyable hours in there with Gunna in duck shooting season. My guess is that, if he doesn't feel safe in his caravan, that's where Gunna will be hiding out."

"Or that's where we'll find the rest of him," I added, thinking of the way the severed arm had flopped in the pug's mouth.

"Don't say that!"

"Sorry. He's a good friend of yours, isn't he?"

"More than that. I've known him for years. Carlton has too, which is why he doesn't like him. Believe it or not, Gunna was our science teacher at high school."

"Really? You're kidding. So how come he's now a swamp-dwelling hermit who may or may not be missing an arm?"

"He retired. He finished teaching the day before his sixty-fifth birthday, packed his stuff and walked away from civilisation. I admire him for following his dreams. Carlton just thinks he's gone senile."

"So, before I die of hypothermia from wet feet, how do we get out to that what-ever-you-called-it to see if he's there or not?"

"Mai-mai. It's called a mai-mai. And I'm still thinking." In answer to his own thoughts, Bruno unslung his rifle and hoisted it to his shoulder, adjusting the telescopic sight as he focussed on the grassy mound. "Damn," he said as he lowered the weapon, "that didn't help. There is a gap in the wall to shoot through but I can't see into it from this side, even through the scope. If he's in there, he's well hidden."

I didn't reply. I was too busy concentrating on trying to restore feeling to my feet which were starting to go numb from the cold. My shoes were completely soaked through and the water had started to seep up my jeans. I stamped my feet, which only made the situation worse as the ground underneath me started to sink. I shivered noisily, which got Bruno's attention.

"I want to go back to the house," I said. "I'm soaked and I'm freezing. How do I get out of here?"

Under the Southern-Man Swanndri jacket there was a gentleman, or there was until he took a good look at me, stripped it off and handed it to me, then it was me under it, revelling in the musky scent of Bruno-worn wool. As I snuggled into it, Bruno gave one lingering glance back to the lake, then led the way back to solid ground.

Chapter 7

I discovered something else about Bruno. He knew how to light a fire. While I unashamedly helped myself to more of Maggie Netherby's clothes - socks, a jersey hand-knitted in a ghastly shade of puce, and a pair of pink, flannelette pyjama pants that were so large I had to tie them on with a cord I stole from one of the bedroom curtains – and used her bathroom to have a long, hot shower, Bruno had been busy. I finally emerged, drying my short, brown hair with a towel, to find the log fire blazing and, in front of it, a rug, two cushions, and two mugs of coffee.

"Wow!" I dropped onto the rug as close to the fire as I could get. "This is nice."

"Thanks." Bruno came out of the kitchen carrying a plate of biscuits and flopped onto a cushion. "It's my apology for getting you so wet and cold. I shouldn't have dragged you down there. I'll go and have another try later but I'll go by myself and leave you up here in the warm."

"And I will let you. I don't think I want to traipse around the reeds in these gorgeous pyjama pants." I held out my arms to show how baggy the jersey was. "I gather Maggie was not a small lady."

"No she wasn't, but she was surprisingly stylish in a unique way. Even in her duck-hunting camo gear she always managed to look as if she was posing for a fashion shoot. They made a strange pair, Maggie and Gunna; physically the complete opposites but, I think, mentally they were on the same page about a lot of things."

"Maggie and Gunna? Were they a couple? That doesn't make sense. If they were, I wouldn't be here sorting her stuff. Gunna would have inherited it. Wouldn't he?"

"No, sorry." Bruno shook his head. "By pair I didn't mean couple. At least, I've never thought of them that way. They were just two rather eccentric people who shared the same views on ecology. They were both ardent conservationists, especially when it came to the birdlife on the lake, but at the same time they both enjoyed hunting and were crack shots with a rifle. Maggie was a retired university lecturer and Gunna was a school teacher, so they enjoyed debating with each other. And she was kind enough to let him park his caravan on her land, in return for which Gunna was her home handyman – not that he ever completed anything."

I swallowed the last of my coffee and stood up.

"Well then, you need to make it your mission to find him and, if he is still alive and just hiding out, bring him back here. At least we can keep him warm and dry. Which reminds me, I need to throw my clothes through Maggie's washing machine – I can't go back to the campground wearing these things."

Bruno glanced at his watch.

"Okay. I have to get back to work anyway. I need to check on Jackson and I have the afternoon clinic today, so I had better get going. I'll come back later and have another go at getting to the mai-mai, but I'll bring my thigh waders and I'll see if I can find you a pair of gumboots. I'm pretty sure Amy will have a spare pare."

Amy. Oh great. I get to wear his girlfriend's gumboots. Super.

"Thanks, that would be awesome," I lied.

I watched him drive away with a disconcerting feeling of domestic contentment that stayed with me as I rinsed our cups then threw my wet clothes into the washing machine. I had to remind myself that we weren't a married couple; I didn't watch him drive away to work as a daily ritual and I certainly didn't then content myself with tidying the house. But that was how I felt. The whole package of the house, the lake, Bruno and me, and Jackson, disconnected my reality and took me to a place in my head that felt more real, even though I knew it was an illusion. I had to physically shake myself and stamp my feet to pull my emotions back into my actual life. Then the guilt kicked in as my work ethic started to nag at me. I imagined my boss's reaction if she found out I had been wandering around the lake when I should have been counting boxes of books. I checked my phone, almost expecting her to have known that I was slacking off and to have sent me a terse text, but there were no messages, not even from Simon. Could he have finally got it through his head that I wasn't coming back? With a sigh of relief, I tightened the cord holding up my pants and stepped through the secret door into Maggie's hoard.

In a fit of enthusiasm I began with the boxes I had already looked at. Without Jackson to worry about, it was easy to prop the front door open and drag them all out onto the deck where I piled them up as high as I could manage without them falling over. By the time Bruno's Land Rover rattled back into the driveway, I had emptied the room, filled the porch and completely covered the sliding doors to the guest bedrooms, leaving just enough space to get down the stairs. I stacked the box I was carrying and watched, puzzled, as Bruno didn't stop but carried on around the back of the house, pulling the vehicle tightly in beside the laundry steps.

"Why have you hidden your truck?" I asked as he emerged around the side of the house, proudly waving a parcel of fish and chips.

"Because, if Carlton turns up tonight, I don't want him to know I'm here."

"Do you think he is going to come back tonight?" I asked as we made ourselves comfortable on the rug, Bruno opening out the fish and chips in front of us.

'Yeah, I reckon he will. He's got to feed those pigs and he knows his mate shot Jackson. I'm surprised he hasn't turned up already."

"So what are you planning to do that's made you hide your truck? Shouldn't we just lock up while it's still daylight and get the hell out of here?"

Bruno sucked seductively on a long, succulent chip and smiled. "Well, I'm not forcing you to stay but I was hoping you'd let me hole up here and keep watch. Plus, I brought my waders, because I want to have another search for Gunna. I'm damn sure he's down at the lake. Oh, and if you do want to join me, Amy did have a pair of gumboots spare."

Amy again. Whenever the mood gets interesting, Amy pops up. I wish she would run away with Carlton. But how can I be jealous of someone I've never met over someone I've only known a day or two. Seriously, Andrea, get a grip!

"Awesome," I faked.

"And I borrowed some overalls from work for you, unless you've become addicted to those exotic pink pyjamas."

At least they weren't borrowed from Amy too. No, that was an ungrateful thought. If I was going to go back down to the lake, overalls and gumboots would be much better than getting my jeans, which I had forgotten about, wet again. I gave myself a mental telling off then thanked Bruno with genuine appreciation.

"How is Jackson?" I changed the subject.

"Doing fine. He's awake and responding to his name. I've given him some more pain medication and tucked him up on a heat pad. He's a good dog. He's tougher than he looks. You've been busy, too. That's quite a pile you've dragged out onto the porch. Are any of the books valuable or are they all destined for the dump?"

"The dump, I'm afraid. Some of those boxes are mouldy and the mice have had a field day in them, so it's not even worth offering them to a second hand book shop, which is where they all seem to have come from in the first place."

"Did you find the gun cabinet behind the boxes?"

"No, I didn't. The room's empty apart from the boxes, although I've only made it through about half of them, so I haven't found the back wall yet, and that's only the first room. There's another just as full. If the cabinet is there, it's probably in the second room. You're welcome to have a look."

"Yeah, I will, if that's okay with you. You're going to need to find the guns for your inventory anyway and I'd be happier if I knew they were all there and still safely locked up." Bruno rolled up the now empty fish and chip wrapping paper, tossed it into the wood burner and stood up. "But, I think I will stick to my original plan and go back down to the lake while it's still light enough to see where I'm going. I don't think the gun cabinet is going anywhere."

"Neither am I," I replied. "Going anywhere, that is. You can yomp off by yourself, because I'm staying here to attack a few more of these boxes or I'll never get back to Wellington."

"Do you want to?"

"Sort more boxes of mouldy books? Oh hell, yeah, I'm having a ball."

"No. Do you want to go back to Wellington?"

"Well... I ..." I had to stop and think. "Actually, no, not really. It's like another world down here. But of course I'm going to have to go back. It's where I live."

Bruno raised his eyebrows, tilted his head and shrugged. "You never know. Things change."

Then he was out the door and gone, leaving me to work out why I found the thought of going home so distasteful. I walked to the window, expecting to see him striding across the paddock, but he had disappeared. Had he fallen? Was he hurt? I peered out the window, my heart racing, then just as I was preparing to rush out the door, I saw him sauntering towards the fence, rubber thigh waders flapping over his shoulder. I stepped back from the window in case he looked up and saw me. How could I have been so stupid? He had told me he had brought his waders and he wasn't wearing them in the house, so of course he had gone to the truck to get them. Why did I panic? Maybe it was time to go back to Wellington.

Telling myself that I was being silly, I still couldn't resist the temptation to look out the window again. Bruno was moving fast, unencumbered by me to slow him down, and was almost at the lake's edge. I watched for several minutes until he stopped to pull on the waders, then turned back into the room and the job I was being paid to do.

It didn't take long to fall back into the rhythm I had developed earlier in the day, so I made good progress, although this time I left the sorted boxes in the room, against a cleared wall, as there was no room left outside on the porch. I quickly got back into the routine I had established before – check for signs of mould or mice, open the box, pull enough out so I could take a look at the ones on the bottom then throw the top ones back in and close the box – so I worked fast and was almost at the back wall when I found the first box of papers.

It looked like all the others when I opened it, another box of second-hand pulp romances, but the books were only two layers deep. Under them I found a pile of transparent plastic files, each one full of hand-written notes. Each file was labelled with the same sort of code I had found on the legs of the stuffed birds in the shed, so I assumed that the files were the details of each piece of taxidermy. But why were they stuffed into a box of romance books, under a pile of other boxes? Why were they not in a filing cabinet or, at least, in a sensible place? I considered stopping to read through them, then decided that could wait. Instead, I repacked the romance novels into another box and carried the box of files through to the lounge so I could look at them later.

Through the lounge window I was surprised to see the light fading. I had spent longer sorting the boxes than I had thought. Where was Bruno? He should have been back by now. Had he fallen in the lake? Should I have gone with him? What was that banging? I hadn't noticed the noise when I was in the secret room but now I could hear a repetitive thudding. Carlton? Was he here? No, it wasn't a rifle. Then it stopped and I heard footsteps. I froze. The feet climbed to the porch but before I went into a full-blown panic attack, I recognised Bruno's voice.

"Hey, Andy, open up. My arms are full."

Laughing at my own stupidity, I opened the door and Bruno entered, carrying a load of firewood that explained the thudding.

"I thought I'd stock up," he said, kneeling to stack the logs beside the woodburner. "It's getting cold out there. I don't suppose the jug's on? I need something warm."

For the next few minutes we could have been any contented couple – Bruno tended to the fire then went to wash his hands while I rummaged in Maggie's pantry and found a can of pumpkin soup which I heated and served in two giant mugs. Bruno took the one I handed to him and flopped down in front of the fire, stretching his legs so that I was forced to step over them to find my own place to sit.

"Did you find Gunna?" I asked as I made myself comfortable on the rug.

"Yes and no. I waded out to the mai-mai and I could tell that he's been there recently, he's made himself a nice little camp, but he wasn't there when I was there. Knowing Gunna, it's possible he wasn't far away and he was probably watching me, but the only living beings I saw were swans and ducks. But I left him a message. I tucked one of my business cards into the reeds that make up the wall. If anyone else sees it, they'll just think some shooter put it there in case they needed a vet urgently, but Gunna will know it's new and realise I was there. He doesn't miss a trick. I'm just hoping he'll have the good sense to get in touch."

"I found something, too, while you were away. That box over there. It had romance novels on the top but underneath them were a whole lot of files, all coded like the dead birds in the shed. I was just going to look through them when you came in."

"Okay. Drag them over here and I'll give you a hand." Bruno looked at his watch. "It'll be a couple more hours before Carlton shows his face, if he's going to; this'll give us something to do while we wait."

"Are you seriously going to tackle Carlton when he turns up to feed those ghastly pigs?"

"Hell, no! I'm going to sneak over to the shed as quietly as possible and take pictures. I'm after evidence that'll stand up in a court. I am going to take that bastard down this time. Speaking of bastards, I meant to ask you earlier – who's Simon?"

"What?" Bruno's change of topic took me by surprise.

"Simon Bastard. In your phone. Sorry, I wasn't prying but way earlier, when we were looking at the photos of the swans, you had a couple of texts come through, which you ignored, but I couldn't help noticing the name. Is there really someone with the last name Bastard?"

"No," I laughed. "His name is Simon Briggs, but he is a bastard, so I changed it. He's my ex. He didn't want me to come down here. I was supposed to stay in Wellington and hang on his arm, but I finally realised what a control freak he was and I left. This job was the perfect opportunity to get away from him. He's been texting me ever since. He even bought me plane tickets so I could fly back to go to his mother's birthday party with him. I cancelled them and I bet he was livid when I didn't get off the plane and fall apologetically into his arms. Before you yomped off, you asked me if I wanted to go back to Wellington and I guess the true answer is no, I am dreading running into him again. I will have to sort out a new place to live when I get back, and change my phone number so he can't find me. At least I know I won't run into him in the Waihola pub."

"He sounds like a real prick. He'd probably get on well with Carlton."

"Oh, bitchy!" We both laughed. "Now, enough about Simon, he is past history. Let's look at these files and see if we can figure out what Maggie was filing away. Oh, hang on," I reached for my inventory that I had left on the couch, "let's check the numbers on the files against the tag numbers on those birds. I wrote them all down with a description of the bird."

Bruno picked the first folder from the box, studied the front page then scanned my inventory list until he found the matching code number. His eyes flicked from one sheet to the other, his concentration creating deep lines across his tanned forehead.

"I've figured out the numbers," he said, flicking his hair from his eyes in his habitual move as he grinned at me. "The first set of letters and numbers are a grid reference that nobody but Gunna and Maggie would understand and the second set of numbers are a date, written backwards - year, month, day, time."

"What's the grid reference to?" I asked.

"The lake. I told you Gunna and Maggie were, are, ardent conservationists. I'm sure Gunna knows every bird on the lake individually. Between them they know which birds are nesting, which areas have the best food. Anything and everything you might need to know about the birds on this lake, Gunna knows. He and Maggie drew themselves a map of the lake and drew a grid over the top of it to make it easier to keep track of things – it's easier to say there's a nest in section R3B than say it's in the patch of reeds just after the fallen tree but before you get to the bend, if you see what I mean. It was purely for their own use."

"Okay, so if the first part is the where , what does the date refer to? The day the bird died?

"Yeah, I think so. That would make sense."

"But, if Gunna and Maggie were such great conservationists, why were they killing the birds and stuffing them?"

"Good question. I don't know. What was that?" Bruno sat straighter, his head cocked to the side.

"What was what?" I asked as Bruno got to his feet, motioning towards the door.

"Shh, someone or something is outside," he whispered. "I heard a footstep on the gravel."

Then I heard it too, only now it was on the steps, followed by a muffled cry and a swear word as whoever it was side-swiped one of the piles of boxes. Bruno moved quickly but without a sound. With hand movements, he indicated that he was going to sneak out the laundry door and make his way around the outside of the house. I stood where I was, rooted to the spot, unable to make my legs propel me anywhere as my flight or fight reaction chose the third option of freeze.

The door shuddered under the weight of the determined knocking. A voice called my name. The freeze spell broke and I sank onto the couch. Surely not. He couldn't have found me here.

"On-dray-a! I know you're in there. Open the damned door immediately. It's bloody cold out here."

From the kitchen Bruno turned and mimed me a message that asked who it was. The act of mouthing back "Simon

Bastard" turned my fear into anger and now it was my fight reaction that kicked in. I strode to the door and flung it open, facing Simon with my arms firmly crossed across my chest. Mustering all the control techniques he had used on me, I kept my voice as calm and as low as I could.

"Get the fuck out of here and piss off back to Wellington."

Behind me I heard the laundry door close.

"Step back and let me in so we can discuss this rationally," Simon blustered. "I'm bloody freezing. Why did you make me come to this godforsaken hole to get you. Why didn't you come home when I told you to. I sent you the ticket. Mother says to tell you it was very rude."

"Tell Mother to get fucked."

"That's enough! I will not have you using such foul language. Now step aside and let me in!"

"No." I straightened my back to give myself as strong a pose as possible, fighting the instinct he had drilled into me to bow my head and apologise. Not this time. "Go away, Simon. We are finished. Over. Defunct. I am not coming back to you, ever. Do you get that? Ever! Now turn around and bugger off."

For a second, Simon looked surprised. I guess he was. In his world people did as he ordered, especially "his woman". Then he got angry. I could see him swallowing back his desire to shout at me. He squeezed his hands together alternately, hand over hand, in a gesture I remembered as part of his technique for channelling his fury so he could deliver it with the cold violence I had come to fear. I held my ground.

"Don't. Be. Ridiculous," he snarled, his voice flat and quiet. "You WILL come back with me. Right now. You will let me in. You will put on some proper clothes. Why on earth are you dressed like that? Have you lost your mind? Then you will get in my car and we will leave. You do not have a choice. I am not giving you one." He took a step towards me, expecting me to step aside and let him in but I didn't move. "Oh, for heaven's sake, On-dray-a, hurry up and get on with it."

"No. What part of no did you not get the first time I said it? Do you ever listen to yourself, you pompous jerk? Look at you in your pin-striped suit and your slicked back hair. How did I ever let myself become so subservient to you? You're a nasty, bullying, abusive psychopath and I am not putting up with your crap anymore."

That was when I made my mistake. I took a step back and relaxed my arms in preparation for slamming the door in his face, but Simon was surprisingly fast. He darted forwards, grabbed the arm I was raising and hauled me towards him, his left hand coming up just as quickly to deliver a sharp slap to my cheek. Then, whatever he was going to say was stopped as his hand was pulled away from my arm and his body swung around. As I raised my hand to feel my stinging cheek, Simon's whole body lifted in front of me and slammed into the doorframe, held in place by Bruno's fierce grip on Simon's pin-striped lapels.

"You heard the lady," Bruno growled, punctuating his sentence by slamming Simon against the door frame between each word. "Get on your bike, Bastard, and don't come back, because if you do, I'll be waiting for you."

Bruno let Simon go but stood between us. Simon tried to muster some authority but failed, his Wellington city bluster overwhelmed by Bruno's natural confidence.

"Who are you?" Simon asked, his normal condescending tone reduced to a plaintive squeak.

Bruno leaned close. "You're worst friggin' nightmare, Sunshine."

Simon pressed himself back against the door frame, terror contorting his elegant face.

"I'm a pig hunter," Bruno continued, "so I know how to slit a throat and butcher a carcass, and I know where to dump a body so it will never be found. Get the message?"

I stepped forwards to stand beside Bruno, pointed up the drive to the road where I assumed Simon had parked his car, and ordered him to leave. I could see his mouth moving as he tried to find the right phrase to give himself the last word but then Bruno gave his knuckles a menacing crack and Simon ran, scuttling down the steps and sprinting up the drive in a turn of sped he normally saved for the squash courts. We waited until we heard the sound of the car's engine before we turned to each other and burst out laughing.

"So that was Simon Bastard," Bruno said as he draped his arm around my shoulders to herd me back into the house. "Nice guy. Not!"

"Thank you." I turned on Bruno's arms and hugged him. "Thank you for pulling him off me. And for scaring the shit out of him. You get the Southern Man Superhero award for the day."

Bruno returned the hug, his embrace warm and comforting, then he pushed me back and gently touched my cheek. "He is never going to hit you again." He looked at me, his expression solemn. "It's not the first time, is it?"

"No, but you're right, it's definitely the last." I reluctantly pulled away from Bruno's embrace and walked to the kitchen, busying myself by filling the jug and spooning instant coffee into mugs. By the time the mugs were ready, my hands had stopped shaking and I had my confused emotions almost in check. I held out a coffee to Bruno and walked past him back to the warm fire, ignoring the fluttering in my breast when our hands touched and the warm feeling that ran through me when he put his arm around my shoulders as we moved into the lounge.

"So tell me more," Bruno asked as we made ourselves comfortable side by side on the couch. "How long have you put up with that prick?"

"Four years. I met him through work. He was buying a property our firm was valuing and I had to deliver some paperwork to his office. The girls in my office were very impressed when he sent me flowers and an invitation to dinner. They all thought he was the perfect catch. So did he. Well, so did I to start with. He seemed so strong and confident, so masterful. I took it as a compliment the first few times he bought me dresses. I was overwhelmed, flattered, that anyone could care so much as to buy me such expensive things. Then things started to change."

"He turned nasty?"

"He certainly did, but slowly and all done so I blamed myself. It was my fault that I said something inappropriate, or used the wrong wine glass, or wore the wrong colour shoes. My friends tried to tell me that I was losing my self-confidence, apologising to him too much, but he was also very good at keeping me away from my old friends and only associating with his business cronies, Apart from work, my life began to completely revolve around him."

"So what made you see the light and leave?"

"Not what, who. My boss, actually, and the girls in the office. The same ones who had thought he was so marvellous. When I turned up to work for the third time with a black eye, they staged an intervention. My boss knew a woman who worked in a women's refuge, so she dragged me off to talk to her. I thought we were going out on a normal job then the next thing, I'm being counselled. It took them a while to convince me that they were right and he was a psychopath but then, a week ago, he told me to wear a green dress but it was a cold night so I wore something else, and he hit the roof."

"He hit you?"

"He wanted to, I could tell, but he had been in a long meeting so I had taken a taxi and met him at the restaurant. I was lucky that it was full of people and Simon would never make a scene in public. He started to vent but realised people were watching so he took his temper out on the poor waiter. As usual, he ordered for me, so I sat there like a meek little lamb, not saying anything, just knowing what was going to come afterwards. Then, all of a sudden, I knew I had to get out of there. I knew he would get up and go to the toilet just before the main course was served, he always did, and as soon as he had gone into the gents, I bolted. I grabbed a taxi, went home, locked the door, turned off the lights and sat in the dark. He turned up about half an hour later, banging on the door and shouting, but I kept quiet and after the neighbour yelled at him to shut up, he went away. And that's about it. He has sent me lots of texts and left messages on my phone ranging from apologetic to threatening, and he has sent several bunches of flowers but my workmates are doing a good job of running interference for me and I'm sure the boss sent me down here to give me some space. I had thought he had finally got the message."

"Let's hope he has now," Bruno growled. "Because I will punch his lights out if he comes back."

I laughed and picked up the folder we had been looking at. "Anyway, enough of him, I am over him and he is a done deal. Let's get back to the birds. Let's look at one that matches a bird in the shed and see what's written about it."

I handed a file to Bruno who started reading until, as he had done before, he stopped and cocked his head to the side.

"No, don't tell me he's come back. Is he stupid or something?"

"Did you hear something? Is Simon still out there?"

"I think so. Let's lock the doors, just to be safe. You check the laundry door, I'll get the front one."

I raced through to the laundry and flicked the lock then rushed back to the couch where I huddled, legs drawn up to my chest, cuddling a cushion. I knew I was being a coward but I was scared. I watched Bruno checking the windows, listening intently to the noises outside, before he came back to reassure me. The noises stopped and we were breathing a sigh of relief when the door to the secret room opened and a figure walked out.

Chapter 8

I screamed. It was a character from a horror movie, covered in mud. Bruno, however, leapt to his feet and grasped the walking scarecrow by his dirty shoulders.

"Gunna! Oh my god, am I glad to see you. Where have you been? Oh boy, you smell bad."

The mud monster stared at me then looked at Bruno for several seconds. I was beginning to think he was mute when he suddenly smiled.

"I got your message. Could I possibly trouble you to let me have a shower as I believe you are undoubtedly correct and I am, indeed, rather malodorous." He held out a backpack he was carrying. "I collected my provisions from the caravan but I have no running water there, and it's been more than a few days since I last had unfettered access to this place. I hope you don't mind."

"Not at all. Let's get you clean and fed and then we can talk. Gunna, this is Andy North. Andy, meet Gunna."

"Pleased to meet you, Gunna. Forgive me if I don't shake hands. You do smell really bad. Go, wash. Would you like some soup? I know there are a few more cans in the pantry."

"Oh, thank you, that would be life-saving."

Gunna disappeared down the hall, leaving Bruno and I to shake our heads in bewilderment.

"Well, at least we know he's alive," Bruno said.

"And both his arms are still attached," I replied.

"So who is the poor bugger in the swan pile?"

"Let's hope Gunna can answer that one."

Bruno nodded in agreement, and I contended myself with silently watching him as he pottered in the kitchen, heating soup and making toast, his face set in the same brow-furrowed frown he had when he was taking the bullet from Jackson's leg. He caught me watching him and asked what I was smiling about, but I was saved from having to answer by the timely arrival of a clean and sweet-smelling Gunna. Without the mud, Gunna still looked like a scarecrow, his slightly-built frame barely filling his ex-military camouflage pants and green woollen jersey, but his shoulder-length, straggly grey hair was clean and his wispy beard was trimmed.

"Ah," he said with obvious pleasure as he held his hands out towards the warmth of the fire. "That feels so much better." He turned to Bruno and I. "Do you mind if I camp in the athenaeum for a few nights? I won't be any bother."

"The where?" I asked at the same time as Bruno asked "The what?"

"The athenaeum." Gunna pointed to the bookcase that was really the door to the secret room. "The rooms behind the bookcase. Maggie and I call it the athenaeum. Wonderful word, means a place where reading materials are kept for study which, as you have seen, is its purpose. But it could also be a very convenient place for me to disappear into for a few days, and it would be a lot warmer and drier than camping in the mai-mai. Very astute of you, Bruno, to have worked out that I was there, by the way. I'm mightily glad Carlton never had your problem-solving skills."

"Did Maggie read all of those books?" I asked.

"Oh heavens, no. Those trashy pulp novels were our interior mai-mai, our duck blind for the curious. All protection for the treasure. I presume you haven't found the sleeping dragon yet."

"I think I have. Maybe you can explain it to us."

"I think there is a hell of a lot more than that to explain," Bruno interrupted. "I think Gunna should start at the beginning and tell us what the hell is going on, who is that poor sod in the woolshed and how come their arm was floating in the lake, wearing your duck caller, Gunna."

Gunna slurped his soup noisily then sat forwards on the couch, resting his elbows on his knees and cradling the warm mug in both hands.

"It's a long story, and it's a real shame Maggie isn't here to help tell it. Most of the work in the sleeping dragon is hers. I did some of the field work, but it was Maggie's brain that put it all together. She was the one who decided to keep track of it all, and to hide the records until we had enough proof to nail the bastards. We were almost there, too. If she had just been more careful, treated that lake edge with more respect, not got so complacent, she'd be the one sitting here telling you this. She should have left old Herman to sort himself out. Silly woman."

"Herman?" I was completely lost and, by the look on his face, so was Bruno.

"The swan," Gunna explained. "Down past my caravan. There's a nest, been there for years, same pair of swans, Herman and Matilda, we called them. Anyway, Maggie and I were planning to meet down there to do our usual check-up. I was already out on the lake in the dinghy when I saw Maggie wading through the weeds. I knew she was getting too close to the swans' nest and I yelled out but she didn't hear me. Deaf as a post. Anyway, old Herman is a grumpy old shit and gets very protective of his nest and he came at her like a raging bull, head down, wings out, flapping and squawking. Poor old Maggie got a dreadful fright, forgot all her training and did exactly the wrong thing. She turned and ran, which made her a perfect target for Herman. I'm paddling like crazy to try to get to Maggie when Herman lunges at her and knocks her over. I can see her trying to get up and protect herself, but he's a big, strong bird and he just kept at her. I still don't know if she fainted or if he knocked her out but by the time I got the dinghy to a landing place, then waded around to her, Maggie was gone. Drowned. In just a few inches of water. I still can't believe it."

"You can't blame yourself." Bruno placed a comforting hand on Gunna's shoulder. "You did all you could in the circumstances."

"Yes, I know," Gunna nodded. "It was just so... needless. It shouldn't have happened. And it has forced my hand. I had been trying to tell Maggie that maybe we should let the whole thing go and mind our own business, but she was so outraged. So I felt obliged to carry on, and now I'm hiding in a duck blind hoping I'm going to live another day."

"Well you don't have to hide in the mai-mai anymore," Bruno said. "It's still Maggie's house so there's no reason why you can't stay here. Is there, Andy?"

"No," I shrugged my shoulders. "I should say no, you can't stay, but, frankly, the last couple of days have been so crazy, I can't think of any reason to stop you. You might even be more entitled to be here than I am. If you don't mind me asking, how come you didn't inherit this place? Why am I here valuing it all for sale if Maggie could have left it to you?"

"Because we were idiots," Gunna acknowledged. "Young

and stupid became old and stupid." He sipped at his soup before continuing. "I met Maggie when I was at teachers' college. She was first year at university, studying zoology, and we both lived in the same hall of residence. We clicked right away and all through our studies we were a couple. Then I got sent to the West Coast on my first teaching placement and Maggie was offered a scholarship to Cambridge to complete her doctorate, so we went in two completely different directions. Both of us got tied up in our new lives and we drifted apart. Then I did the unthinkable, in Maggie's eyes. I met a local girl in Greymouth and married her. Maggie never forgave me. My marriage didn't work out and we separated years ago, long before I met Maggie again, but that wasn't good enough. Maggie wasn't interested in getting married, said she wasn't being my second choice and, anyway, technically we couldn't as I've never got around to filing divorce papers so I'm still legally married to Sandra. So we've let all the old history get in the road. We never did what we should have done years ago and now it's too late. I'll just have to hope that whoever buys this place is kind enough to let me keep my caravan parked down at the lake. I've kind of got used to being one with the swans. I don't think I could live in a real house again, especially if it wasn't this one."

The sadness in Gunna's voice left me bereft. My job was usually so impersonal, I just listed items on a clipboard and tallied up their value, but Gunna's loss was invaluable, his whole world had crumbled in an instant and there was no way I could quantify his loss on my job-sheet. I looked up and realised Bruno was also struggling to find suitable words to respond, so I changed the topic.

"So whose arm is it?"

"I don't know," Gunna answered.

"But it's got your duck caller tied to its wrist," Bruno argued. "Your caller, your handmade caller that everybody recognised and nobody else owns. If you don't know who the arm belongs to, how did the caller get there? Do you randomly tie callers to dead people that you find floating in the lake? Or did you kill him? And if you did, why did you leave your caller on him? And why did you cut his arm off?"

"All fair questions, young Bruno," Gunna smiled. "And when you stop to draw breath and give me some talking space I can answer some of them." With a grin Bruno spread his arms wide in a gesture of surrender as Gunna continued. "To some extent I did tie my caller to a random body, although it wasn't floating when I found it."

"It's in the woolshed, isn't it?"

"One point to Bruno. Yes, indeed. Do I assume you've seen the rest of it then?"

Bruno answered by pulling out his phone and showing Gunna the pictures of the pile, including the skull and the blue material. "So you don't know who he is?"

"I don't have a name but he's one of them. I'd seen him a couple of times, doing business with them at the shed, but I don't know his name and I don't even know if he was a supplier or a buyer, but I know they argued about money and I know Carlton was pretty damned angry when his mate blew that bloke away."

"How do you know? Were you there?"

"I was close. That old woolshed is derelict. There are lots of holes in the wall on the far side that Carlton hasn't bothered to patch because he thinks nobody can see in as there are no houses overlooking it, but there is a wonderful macrocarpa hedge two paddocks up the road. I've built a lovely blind in it which, with my binoculars, gives me a perfect view inside the shed. It's like sitting in the gods at the opera. And almost as entertaining some nights. Anyway, last week, so that's nine or ten nights ago, I was positioned in my tree, all nicely furnished with a thermos of tea and a box of sandwiches, as I was expecting them to be making a deal, and I watched the whole thing play out in all its technicolour gore."

Gunna paused to finish his soup then took up his tale.

"As usual, it was nearly dark when Carlton and his ugly thug of a mate, Nettles, arrived. I saw them coming up the road then, about five minutes later, the other bloke drove up. I saw them open the boots of both cars then I saw them carrying dead swans into the shed but, because of the angle, I couldn't make out which car they had come out of, which is why I said I didn't know if that bloke was bringing birds to sell to them or buying meat off them, or both. Whichever, they took a dozen birds into the shed then came outside and lit cigarettes. Then the shit hit the fan. The bloke said something and Carlton got angry. They were yelling at each other so loudly, I could hear enough of it to know it was the price of the birds they were arguing over, but I'm not sure if Carlton wanted to pay less, or wanted the bloke to pay more. After a few minutes of yelling, the bloke turned to walk away and Carlton ran after him, spun him round and punched him. The bloke went down for a second or two then came up fighting and the two of them went hammer and tongs at each other. By the time the bloke managed to get the better of Carlton and knock him out, they were both on their last legs. Carlton slumped to the ground in a heap and the bloke pulled himself up and started to stagger back to his car. I guess he was going to cut his losses and get the hell out of there. Anyway, just as he was getting to his car, Nettles storms around the building with his rifle and shot the bloke in the head. One shot, stone dead."

Bruno leant forwards to throw another log onto the fire and we all watched the flames flare brightly before Gunna continued.

"By that time, Carlton was coming round and he was not best pleased with Nettles, that's for sure. I could see that he was furious but I couldn't hear them. There was a lot of waving of arms and angry pointing, then Nettles dragged the bloke's body into the shed. I wanted to know what they were doing but I wasn't stupid enough to get near until they were well and truly gone, then I climbed down out of my tree, sneaked across the paddock and climbed in through the rotten wall. The top level of the shed was empty but I knew about the trapdoor so I figured they had chucked the bloke down it. And I was right. I went down to the bottom and there he was, all butchered up with the swans."

"Weren't you scared of the pigs?" I asked.

"They weren't there then. Nettles brought them in the next day. Good way to get rid of a body, pigs. They'll eat everything except the hair, which didn't matter with this bloke because he was bald."

"Hang on," I interrupted. "Are you saying they brought those pigs in specially to eat that guy's body?"

"I reckon. Which is why I'm glad I grabbed his arm when I had the chance."

"Why did you?" Bruno asked. "Why didn't you just report it?"

"To whom would I report it, young Bruno?" Gunna sounded like the teacher he had once been. "The police? The local policeman? Oh wait, that's Carlton. No, Bruno, if I had reported it, Carlton would have found a way to twist it back on me. He knew Maggie and I were aware of his game and, with Maggie no longer here, he'd find it very easy to set me up and get rid of me too."

"Which is why you disappeared and have been hiding out," I said.

"Yes. I was struggling to work out the best thing to do. I saw the bloke's arm sticking out of the pile and, as I reached for it, I noticed my duck caller hanging on my wrist. That gave me the idea. I knew people would know it was my caller and I also knew it wouldn't take long for them to work out that it wasn't my arm. I figured that, if it became a proper forensic investigation and a full-on hunt for the rest of the body, then Carlton wouldn't be able to cover it up."

"I still don't get why the duck caller," Bruno said. "Wouldn't the arm be enough? Why connect yourself to it when you could have just floated the arm in the lake then waited at the pub to see who found it? Wasn't putting your caller on it just helping Carlton to crucify you?"

"That was a calculated risk, and one I have regretted taking several times since, but it made sense in the heat of the moment. I was counting on there being enough people in Waihola who cared about me to make a fuss. If it was just a random arm, there was a chance it could be passed off as a freak boating accident and Carlton would sweep it under the covers as quickly as possible. I had to do something to make people take notice and my duck caller was the only thing I could think of at the time."

"Well, it has certainly worked," Bruno said. "Everybody is talking about you, wanting to know if the arm is yours, where is the rest of you, are you alive or lying somewhere injured. Carlton is rushing around pretending to care and desperately hoping he will find you before anyone else does. I wouldn't go near your caravan for a while, if I was you. Stay here, keep out of sight and I will bring supplies. But you'd better keep the place locked and the lights off when Andy's not here."

"I've got an idea," I suggested. "I could check out of the motor camp and move in here. I can tell them there is so much to sort, it's easier to stay here. Then it won't matter if anyone sees lights on because they'll think it's me."

"Good idea," Bruno nodded in agreement. "Look, I know I was hoping to catch Carlton over there tonight but, with all that Gunna had just told us, I think it's more important for us to sit and make some plans. What do you guys think?"

"I agree," I said. "Let's take a break. Let's find the linen and make some beds up. It could be a long night. Unless you need to get back to the clinic, Bruno."

"No, I'm right. I had already organised cover for emergencies and for Jackson, so I don't need to be back until my clinic tomorrow afternoon."

"Jackson?" Gunna gasped. "Is he all right? Why is he at the clinic?"

"Nettles shot him," Bruno explained, "but he's okay. He'll be limping for a while but he's doing well. Andy might be able to bring him home tomorrow."

"Here?" A smile lit up Gunna's face. "I've missed that little guy. I thought I had lost him forever."

I was confused again. "So why did he end up in the pound? Why didn't you just go and pick him up?"

"Me, making bad choices again. I was distraught when Maggie died. I wasn't thinking straight. I wasn't even feeding myself, let alone Jackson and he ran away. The neighbours found him and handed him on to the ranger but it was a few days before I found out where he was. Then I had to deal with the funeral and a few more days went by. When I did contact the ranger, she wasn't too impressed that it had taken me so long to get in touch with her and she kind of pressured me into giving him up, telling me she would find him a loving home with a family when all I could offer was a damp caravan. If I had been in a better headspace I would have told her to go to hell and brought him home, but I didn't. I've thought about him every day since, wondering where he went. I thought he had been rehomed already. How come he was anywhere Nettles could shoot him?"

"He was here, with me," I replied. "The ranger handed him over to me. I was going to take him to a rescue organisation, but it took about five minutes to fall in love with him, so I'm keeping him. He'll be coming back to Wellington with me when I finish here." I felt guilty when Gunna's smile faded. "Or maybe he can stay here with you. I'm not sure how I would manage a dog in the city anyway."

To cover the tears I could see misting his eyes, Gunna bustled down the hall to the linen cupboard and came back with a pile of sheets and blankets which he doled out to Bruno and me. Clutching our bundles, we followed obediently as he allocated us our bedrooms, giving me Maggie's master bedroom at the back of the house and sending Bruno to the guest room that overlooked the deck before he stepped through the bookcase-door to make up his own sleeping arrangements.

I felt like an intruder in Maggie's room but, at the same time, I felt I was at home. Maggie's extensive use of gold trim and burgundy velvet made the room look like a movie set for a B-grade film but it drew me in with an unexpected feeling of warmth and comfort. I took my time making the oversized bed, then sat on it, imagining curling up under the covers. Then my imagination added Bruno to the picture and I snapped out of my daydream, angry with myself for my thoughts. I was glad his bedroom was at the other end of the house, with Gunna between us. To shake off my musing, I looked around the room, taking in the overwhelming rococo styling. Bruno was right, Maggie's taste could only be described as unique. In one corner, where I had bundled them as I had checked them onto my inventory list, I saw Maggie's ornaments and knick-knacks piled in a box and I was relieved that Gunna hadn't come into the room to see them looking like discarded rubbish. My business efficiency suddenly seemed like an insult to Maggie's memory and to Gunna's emotions. To assuage my guilt, I pulled a matched pair of china ballerinas from the box and sat them back on the dresser before firmly closing the door on my thoughts and rejoining the men in the lounge.

"So, let's recap," Bruno said as he handed us each a mug of coffee. "Let's get all our ducks in a row. Gunna, I'm impressed. I didn't realise that you and Maggie were aware of Carlton and his little business, although if I had thought about it, I should have worked it out. After all, nobody knows more about the lake than you two. I wish I had known earlier, we could have pooled our resources a month or two ago, but we're here now. I've been trying to collect concrete evidence but I don't know who the buyers are and the suppliers are keeping pretty tight-lipped, even though they are all hunting buddies of mine. They all know I'm not Carlton's best friend and I think they assume that, because I'm the vet, I'm too much of a goody-two-shoes to get into anything illegal. Which is true, but I've been trying to convince them that it's not so they will let me in and give me something I can use as proof."

"I've got the proof," Gunna replied. "Pages and pages of it. All hidden away in the athenaeum under innocent boxes of rubbish. We've got dates, times, numbers of birds, collateral damage to other birds, hell, we've even got photos of some of the deals being done. The only thing we haven't got one hundred percent, is proof of the end product. The best we've managed to get is proof of a delivery to the restaurant and one of our mates has got proof that the meat they ate there was swan. He's a scientist so he bagged some and had it DNA tested, but we don't have any physical proof that links the two together."

"Woah!" I interrupted. "Back the truck up. Restaurant? Are you saying Carlton is getting swans from the lake and selling them to a restaurant? Aren't they protected?"

"Exactly," Gunna nodded. "Our friendly local policeman is breaking the law he is sworn to protect, in a nice little racket that contravenes two different Acts of Parliament. First off, he's committing offences, or getting his mates to commit offences, under the Wildlife Act. That's the act that says what animals can be hunted and what are protected. There are two rules for swans. White swans are totally protected, you can't hunt them at all. Black swans can be hunted but only during the duck shooting season, which we're not in at the moment."

"So all those swans in that pile in the woolshed have been illegally killed?" I asked.

"Yep," Bruno confirmed. "Every one of them." He pulled out his phone and flicked to the photos. "And, although a lot of the white feathers in the pile will be from the black swans' wings, it looks like some of the birds are mutes, so Carlton must have a supplier from Canterbury or someone around here is breeding them."

"Mutes? What? Swans who don't make a noise?" I was baffled.

"No," Gunna answered. "Mutes are white swans. That's what they're called. They're only found wild in a couple of places in the South Island, Lake Ellesmere and North Canterbury, so he must be getting them from a private pond, or even a town's botanic gardens. And they are totally protected, there's no hunting season for them at all, so if there are any in that pile there's no question about them not being illegally caught. Anyway, no matter where they're coming from, or what type of swan they are, he's still not allowed to sell them on to a restaurant. That's the other law he's breaking, the Animal Products Act. Places that sell food have to ensure that food is safe, they can't just buy meat from any old hunter who turns up with a dead bird or pig. They have to buy from certified suppliers. But, wherever you find food, you'll find those self-professed connoisseurs who like to brag about their last meal and have to out-do each other at their next dinner party."

"Sounds like my ex and his mother," I snorted derisively.

"Told you he'd get on well with Carlton," Bruno's laugh made me smile but it didn't stop Gunna who had picked up the papers I had left on the couch and forgotten.

"It's all in here," he said. "Dates, times, the whole lot. Maggie and I kept watch, turn about. It didn't take much to work out who his main suppliers were and, with a bit of help from those young lads from the garage, we've been watching them."

"The Atkins boys are helping you?" Bruno asked.

"Don't sound so incredulous, Bruno," Gunna chastised. "They're good boys. A little wild yet, but they're young. There was a stage I was worried Carlton might turn them to the dark side, but they're smarter than they look, those two."

"Yes they are. I know they've been patrolling the lake, trying to catch that night shooter who's been firing off lately.'

"I heard that – scared the shit out of me," I said. "I thought it was you, Bruno, because I saw you the next morning, loading dead birds into your truck."

"And I was, but only because the boys let me know but they couldn't get down there themselves. Whoever it is likes shooting them but he doesn't bother to retrieve them, just leaves them in the lake. I wish we could catch him."

"My bet's on Nettles," Gunna said. "But don't worry, the Atkins boys will get the proof. They make excellent spies. They've brought me more information on Carlton's suppliers than I could ever have hoped for. I was just after proof of the swan kills but they brought me proof that he's selling wild pig too."

"So the act about selling meat covers pig hunters too?" I clarified.

"Yes, indeed. Meat for sale has to be killed and processed at a certified abattoir, which that old woolshed certainly is not."

"So what do we do next?" Bruno asked. "What's our plan

going to be?"

"Well," I tapped the paper Gunna was holding, "Let's round up all of Gunna's proof. Gunna, this looks like the secret code from a spy movie. Can you please write down a clear explanation of how it works, so whoever we pass it to can understand it? Bruno, you need to make copies of those photos and save them to a couple of different places so we don't lose them. In fact, start by bluetoothing them to my phone and I'll save them to my cloud account. I'll add the ones I took of the pigs."

"Yep, onto it," Bruno acknowledged. "Gunna, are you okay finding those papers yourself? Because if you are, I would like to go back up to the woolshed. I know it's dark but there's a decent moon out tonight and I really want to get a better look at what's in there."

"One thing at a time, Bruno, lad. Let's put that off a few more hours and wait until the sun's coming up. Nothing over there is going anywhere in the meantime. I agree with Andy, the best thing to do now is pull the dragon out of the athenaeum. Come on, we're looking for boxes labelled cat food, or crushed pineapple. If it's any other kind of box, it's not part of the dragon and not important."

"I wish I'd known that a couple of days ago," I muttered, thinking of all the boxes I had ripped open to find them full of pulp trash.

Even with three people, it still took an hour to sort through the last of the boxes in the first room and all the boxes in the second one. We worked as a chain gang, Gunna identifying each box and passing it to Bruno who weaved his way through the maze to hand them to me. My job was to stack them in the first room, rubbish on one side, files by the door. By the time we had finished and lugged twenty boxes of files back to the lounge, I was exhausted. I glanced at my watch, shocked at how late it was.

"That's it. Enough. We're all going to bed," I ordered. Neither man objected so I left them for the comfort of Maggie's massive bed where I quickly fell asleep imagining I was running my fingers over Bruno's face on the pillow beside me.

Chapter 9

I'm not sure if the men got any sleep at all but when I awoke, dressed – in my own jeans instead of Maggie's pyjamas – and headed to the kitchen, I found a scene of domestic bliss. Gunna was sitting on the couch, papers strewn all around him, munching on a piece of toast, while Bruno was standing at the stove solemnly cooking bacon and eggs. I paused in the doorway to admire the picture of perfection as the sun streamed through the window to frame his chiselled cheek bones and sparkle highlighted streaks of gold in his tousled hair.

"Good morning," I said as I stepped into the kitchen's homely warmth. "Did I sleep in or have you two been up all night?"

"No and no," Bruno laughed, his frown lines disappearing as a smile flashed all the way to his eyes. "No, you didn't sleep in, it's only seven o'clock, and no, we haven't been up all night – we grabbed a couple of hours sleep but we got up again at daybreak and we've already been over to the woolshed and taken a heap more photos. Oh, and Gunna knows who the pigs belong to, so we can do Carlton for stealing them too."

"I thought they were wild pigs? They were great, big, hairy things. Domestic pigs are pink, aren't they?"

"Not always," Gunna interjected. "You're thinking of the Landrace breed, but there are other breeds of pigs and a lot of them are black or black and white. In the case of those mongrels up in the woolshed, you're half right – they belong to Hans van Rooy, an old Dutch bloke who lives right up at the end of the road. He's been crossbreeding Berkshires, which are black with white feet, with wild pigs for a few years now. Don't ask me why, it always seemed like a daft scheme to me, but it keeps him happy and, I think Bruno would agree with me, the meat from them is mighty tasty."

"It certainly is," Bruno agreed, handing me a plate of bacon that made my mouth water at its delicious smell. "Try this and see if you agree."

"What? Is this from one of the pigs over there? Did you kill them?" I looked at the plate, unsure if I wanted to take it, in spite of how good it looked and how hungry I suddenly felt.

"No, you duffer," Bruno laughed, pushing the plate towards me. "This is last month's vet bill. Cousin to this month's bill that you met on the back of my truck."

"I'm not following you. Is this safe to eat?"

"Yes it is, don't panic. But it does come from the same place as those pigs in the shed. Old Hans used to make most of his money as a lumberjack but now his eyesight's failing and he can't work a chainsaw safely anymore, so he struggles to make ends meet these days. I help him out with his animals when I can, but he can't afford to pay me cash, so he pays me in pork instead. That beast you saw when we first met, in such ungallant circumstances, was his payment for some surgery I did on one of his dogs that was hurt by a boar."

"And you sold it on to Tom at the camp?"

"Well," Bruno looked sheepish, "that wouldn't be strictly legal, so let's just say Tom owed me money for ... something ... and I gave him a pig as a gift, and it was really useful of him to pay me back right then when I needed to match cash in with expenses out for the surgery's accountant. Okay? Oh, and before you ask, yes, Bill at the pub made some of it into pork pies but no, they are not the ones he sells at the pub. That would be illegal. These ones are just shared between friends around the family table."

"Okay," I laughed, "but can't Carlton make the same excuse?"

"No," Gunna piped up from the couch. "Not when he's dealing in protected species, and selling to a restaurant. Plus, he's a cop and it's not just one pig every now and then, it's a lucrative little business he's got going. Not to mention, he has now covered up the cold-blooded killing of whoever that poor bastard was. So eat up, you lot, we need to get this show on the road."

I settled myself at the dining table, where I was joined by Bruno carrying a plate piled even higher than my over-filled one. In his other hand he carried a plastic tomato from which he poured an extravagant amount of tomato sauce before offering it to me. I declined, then turned back to Gunna.

"So, what's the plan?"

"Gunna's been sorting his files," Bruno began as he chewed a mouthful of bacon.

"Don't talk with your mouth full," Gunna chastised. "But, as he said, I've been organising my paperwork and I have here a small file, which is only the tip of the iceberg but should be enough to prove our point conclusively in our initial discussions and force some action from the authorities. So, as soon as you two are ready, I suggest we embark. Time is a-wasting."

"Where are we embarking too?" I asked. "As Carlton is a cop, we can hardly go to the police, can we?"

"Yes, that's exactly where we are going, but we are going way over Carlton's head," Bruno explained. "Waihola is officially part of Clutha County, so he's based out of Balclutha, so we are going into Dunedin which, of course, is Otago, so it's a different jurisdiction. Hopefully there we can talk to someone who will take us seriously."

"What do you want me to do?" I asked.

"You can be our red herring," Bruno said. "We don't want to risk Carlton realising anything is up and getting rid of that gruesome pile of evidence in his shed, so we were wondering if you could come up with a distraction to keep him busy. I thought maybe you could get him to meet you at the campground and you could make a formal complaint about Jackson being shot. Then keep him talking for as long as you can."

"Easy. I'm sure I can do that. I'll invite him for coffee and bat my eyelashes."

"Right, let's get on our bikes." Gunna stood up, collected his papers together and thrust some of them into a box labelled crushed pineapple. As Bruno and I hurriedly finished our breakfast, Gunna pushed the rest of the papers into several other boxes, carried them through the secret door, then returned carrying a grey army-surplus blanket.

"Can't be too careful," he explained. "Even at this hour of the day there will be a few people up and around and I don't want to be seen yet so, until we get a fair way past the lake, I'll be curled up on the seat of the truck with this over me. I figure it'll be safe to pop up once we get to Allenton."

"How long do you think you will be?" I asked. "So I have

an idea how long I need to keep Carlton distracted."

Bruno looked at his watch and did some mental calculations.

"Give us half an hour's head start, then drive down to the campground. The police station opens at eight, and I'm betting that he'll go there first in the morning. Ring him from the camp and try to get him to come to you mid-morning, then talk slowly."

"I was planning on fast but unintelligibly, so I have to keep repeating myself."

"Perfect! Right, Gunna, let's make tracks."

"After you, Bruno, my lad, after you."

Carrying the blanket and his box of files, Gunna led the way out the door. I waved through the window as they disappeared around the side of the house, then busied myself washing the dishes, pretending I wasn't concerned as I heard them drive away. I checked my watch, calculating when I could leave too, then made coffee and pottered around, filling in the minutes with frequent checks of my watch to see how much time had elapsed. Every mundane task I found to do, straightening the bed, collecting towels and throwing in them in the washing machine, all promised to be activities that would use up the minutes, but the reality was frustratingly different, as each re-check of my watch showed. Time crawled, but the nearer it eventually got to my thirty-minute deadline, the more pointless my attempts to fill the minutes became. I made a second cup of coffee, then tipped it down the sink as I was too nervous to drink it. I wasted a minute staring at my watch, counting the seconds as they ticked off. I walked through the house again, double-checking that all the doors and windows were securely locked, and completed the exercise twice more in a futile attempt to calm my nerves, before sitting on the couch, alternately clapping my hands and slapping them against my knees in time to the seconds as I counted them off.

With five minutes still to go before my deadline, I couldn't bear the enforced waiting any longer. I had to move. With a final check of my watch, I picked up my car keys and my jacket, locked the door and walked to my car. I justified my actions on the grounds that I could drive slowly and it would be easier to fill in time chatting with Gail at the campgrounds but, really, my nerves had reached a point where I just couldn't sit still any longer. Butterflies flipped in my stomach as I fastened my seatbelt. Where were Bruno and Gunna? Were they nearly in Dunedin? Had they passed Green Island? Were they heading over the hill into Caversham? I blew out my tension in a long, whistling sigh as I pulled out of the gate and began my part of the plan.

By the time I had reached the campground, parked my car and checked my cabin, it was almost time to make my phone call to the police station, so I walked over to the office where I found Gail giving directions to an elderly couple in a camper van. I waited until they had left before asking if I could use the office phone and explained why. I didn't add that I still didn't want to use my cell phone in case Carlton recognised my number from my untimely call in the woolshed. Fortunately, Gail was so concerned that I hadn't reported Jackson's accident that she didn't think to ask. Instead, she dialled the police station number herself then handed me the phone. A female voice answered then transferred me to another line.

"Senior Sergeant Ian Carlton speaking."

"Hi. It's Andy North here. Are you going to be in Waihola at all today? I need to report an incident that happened the other night and I was wondering if I can talk to you about it." I knew I was babbling, partly because that was part of my cover plan but also partly because I was nervous. "I'd rather not have to come down to Balclutha as I'm flat out at the Netherby place, my god she had a lot of stuff, but if you're going to be up here, then maybe we can make a time to meet."

"An incident? What happened?"

"My dog was shot."

"You have a dog?" Carlton sounded incredulous. "I didn't see one with you the other night. Was it in your car?"

"No, I got him the next day. Then he ran away and someone shot him. He's going to be okay but I want to make an official report. My insurance company will need a police report number for my claim to be accepted." That was pure invention but I hoped it sounded credible.

"Oh, all right. It's something that happens out in the country and most people wouldn't bother making a complaint, but if you're determined, and if getting down to Balclutha is too much of a hassle, I guess I could come up to the house later."

"Not the house, no. I'm actually in Waihola at the campground this morning. I needed to talk to the garage about Maggie's fancy car, and I have a few other things to sort out here." I was rapidly realising that my ability to tell lies was abysmal and I was falling into my own holes. I was too busy at the house to go to Balclutha but then I wasn't actually at the house. Oh my god, I was confusing myself. Time to wrap this call up. "So, can I meet you at the pub? I'll even buy you a pork pie on my expense account."

"That's a bribe I will happily accept," Carlton laughed. "Let's see, we've got a staff meeting here in a few minutes and that could take a while, then I have to deal with the paperwork on some stolen lawnmowers, so how about we meet at ten thirty? I'll be ready for that pork pie by then."

"Ten thirty sounds perfect. I'll see you then."

As I replaced the receiver on the campground phone, my own phone pinged in my pocket. I didn't recognise the number but the message, *reached police station walking in now*, showed it had to be from Bruno. I texted back a thumbs up sign followed by *meeting C 10.30*, shoved my phone back in my pocket and turned to Gail who had been hovering behind the counter, pretending to be straightening a shelf of canned goods.

"Come on through to the house," she beckoned. "I'll make us a cuppa and you can tell me all about poor little Jackson. What happened to him?"

As Gail led the way to her kitchen and bustled about making us tea, which was so strong I struggled to swallow it, I gave her edited highlights of Jackson's ordeal, with no mention of Carlton or the woolshed. By the time she had mulled the story over in her head and come up with several plausible possibilities, I almost believed myself that Jackson had been shot by a random night shooter out looking for rabbits. Having assured her that Jackson was out of danger, I purposefully changed the topic to the identity of the floating arm, reminding myself before I spoke that I wasn't supposed to know where Gunna was.

"Have they said anything yet? Is it Gunna's arm?" I asked, hoping I sounded genuine.

"Huh," Gail snorted. "Everybody's talking but nobody's saying anything. Nobody has seen Gunna, alive or dead, so half of the pub regulars think it's him and the rest of him will float to the surface soon, but a couple of people from the duck sanctuary reckon they saw Gunna at the other end of the lake. They said it was just a glimpse and they couldn't be certain, but they know him well and they were sure it was him, so maybe he's still alive, but if he's down there with an arm missing, he's not going to last long."

"What about the police? Have they said anything?"

"Not to us, no. Maybe you can get some information out of Ian when you met him."

"I'll try my best." It would keep him talking for a bit longer, even if I already knew more than he did. For safety, I changed the topic again to more general campground gossip and Gail responded by enthusing over how full the camp was going to get as the weekend approached.

"Do you have any idea yet how long you will need your cabin for?" she asked with a hint of apology in her tone. "It's not that I want to kick you out or anything but..."

"You've got bookings that could use it?" I finished for her. As she nodded, I solved both our problems. "Tell you what, if I can still pop in for a chat, I will check out and move my stuff up to the Netherby house. That way I can work as late as I want to, I can look after Jackson when he comes back from the vets, and you can use the cabin for other guests."

I didn't add that my presence at the house would cover Gunna, who could hide out in safety, and I was relieved that I could leave the campground without feeling I had let Gail down. Although she tried to hide it, I could see Gail was pleased by my offer, so I let her lead the way back to the office where I officially signed out, handing over my work's credit card to pay the bill, then I went back to the little cabin and packed my few possessions into my car. I still had time to kill before my meeting with Carlton, so I decided to keep my story straight, and achieve something I was being paid to do. I drove out of the campgrounds, across the road to the garage where I found one of the J boys behind the counter.

"Oh hi," I said, not game to add a name as I still wasn't sure which one was which.

"Hi. I hear you've got Jackson," he began. "Can we have him?"

"Sorry," I replied. "It took me about a minute to fall in love with him. Besides, he's at the vets – did you hear he was shot?"

"What? Who?" The J boy sounded genuinely distressed and continued to utter oaths and threats as I told him the official story, not the real one. "I hope they catch the bastard," he ended. "Just let me at him when they do."

"You'll have to stand in line behind Bruno and Gail," I said. "Anyway, I came in to get advice on Maggie Netherby's vintage car. Where's the best place to have it valued? Can you help me with that?"

"Yeah, there is one guy." J scratched his head as he searched his memory. "I haven't got a contact for him but the rugby club will. Actually, Sergeant Carlton will know, too, they're good mates. I'm not sure if it's his real name or a nickname but he's known as Nettles. He'd be the man to talk to, he's all into his vintage cars. You might want to get a second opinion on the value though, because he's going to offer to buy it. He's been trying to get Maggie to sell it to him for years. As soon as Maggie's funeral was over, he was telling people he was going to make sure he got the car."

"So he's not really the right one to ask about it then?" I laughed.

"Nah, probably not," J agreed. "He was just the one who sprang to mind. Look," he pulled his mobile phone from his pocket, "give me your phone number and I'll text you some better options."

"Okay. I'll grab your number, too, then I'll know who it is when you text me, and I can let you know when Jackson's home again."

"Home, eh?" J picked up on my use of the word. "Settling in up there, are you? Wouldn't blame you if you did. It's a crazy house but it's cool."

I left J, drove back over the road and parked beside the pub, then sat for a few minutes in the car, sorting out my story for Carlton and wondering if Bruno and Gunna were having any success with the police in Dunedin. A failed attempt at a deep breathing exercise to control my nerves made me think of Simon. He had disappeared with his tail between his legs so quickly. I wondered what story he had made up for his mother. I would be branded as every type of cheap whore, Bruno would be a brutal thug, and mother would agree that darling Simon was better off without me, but he would still be seething and I didn't think I had seen the last of him. The J boy had been right, I was starting to feel more comfortable in the Netherby house than I was in Wellington.

A fist knocked on my car window. Broken out of my reverie, I jumped and let out a squeak before realising it was Carlton, smiling at me.

"Sorry, didn't mean to scare you but you were miles

away," he said as I opened the door to join him.

"Yeah, I was," I agreed. "Is that the time? Let's go inside and I will shout you that pie."

In the comfort of the pub, sitting opposite him with hot coffee and steaming pork pies on the table between us, Carlton didn't look anything like the villain he had become in my mind. If his rugby jersey had shown off his immense upper-body muscles, his official police uniform added a layer of don't-mess-with-me that was comforting rather than menacing. I could see why the locals loved him. Especially when he smiled. Bruno and Gunna were going to have a hard job convincing anyone that behind the facade he was running a criminal operation.

Following my prepared script, I rambled in my story about Jackson, pausing to eat so I gained time while I was chewing, intentionally repeating myself and adding bits of information that were completely irrelevant. I could see Carlton wishing I would get on with it; his face fixed in a benevolent smile he probably used on confused old ladies. When we got to the actual shooting, he asked if I had seen anybody and I used my best acting skills to convince him that I hadn't but wished that I had. I told him that I was looking in the garage when I heard the shot, then found Jackson several minutes later.

"Did you hear any vehicles?" he asked, hiding his relief well when I said, "No."

He gave me a form to fill in and sign, which I did slowly enough that he ordered us more coffee while he patiently waited for me to finish. As I handed the form back I sneaked a quick glance at my watch before asking him about the severed arm.

"Have they identified it yet?"

"No. And we haven't found Gunna yet either. It won't be long though. He has to turn up somewhere."

"Gail says the rugby team's taking bets on how long it will be before the rest of him floats up."

"Yeah," Carlton smiled. "I've got $20 on Friday morning."

"Oh, yuk!"

"Well, if that's all, thank you for the pie. I will get this report written up for you and send you the details you need for your insurance. To be honest, I doubt we will find the culprit and if the dog's going to be okay, I don't think we'll be chasing it too hard, but it was good of you to let us know. Are you going to be staying up at the house for much longer?"

I noticed how he had thrown the question in casually.

"Not too much longer, I hope, but a few more days anyway. There is a lot more stuff to value than I expected. The car, for starters. I didn't expect to find a pristine vintage in the garage. Now I have to get it valued and get someone to organise its sale."

"I might be able to help with that," Carlton offered. "I've got a mate who's been after it for years. Do you want me to get him to call up and look at it?"

"Um," I stalled as the thought of Nettles coming anywhere near me made my heart race. "The valuation has to be done by a registered valuer, but, tell you what, I'll let you know when it's going to be sold and you can pass the information on to him. Thanks for meeting me today. I feel reassured knowing that I've officially reported the shooting."

"Right, any time," Carlton forced a smile as he shook my hand and departed.

I felt shattered, the pork pie that had tasted so delicious

refusing to settle in my stomach. I had done my part, successfully keeping Carlton occupied for longer than we had planned. I sat quietly, lingering over the last of my coffee, my thoughts racing and jumping from Carlton to Simon, to Bruno, to Wellington, from the interior of my tiny apartment to the crazy secret rooms of Maggie's house. The uninspiring sight of the building next door that greeted me out my Wellington windows sprang to mind, no comparison to the stunning view from Maggie's kitchen.

A text from Bruno saying they were on their way broke me out of my reverie. With faked cheerfulness, I placed my empty cup on the counter, thanked the bartender who exhorted me to have a nice day, and stepped back out into the sunshine. Even though the wind had a chilly edge, the Waihola air was still sweeter and cleaner than inner-city Wellington on its best day. I breathed deeply, squared my shoulders and pulled my thoughts back to reality, which meant shopping for supplies.

In the dairy I grabbed bread, soup and milk, aware all the time that I was being surreptitiously watched by the woman behind the counter and a second woman leaning on the front of it. I faked my smile again and carried on browsing, listening as they gossiped about the possibility of Gunna rising from the dead or floating in on the high tide.

"He hasn't turned up at Maggie's, by any chance?" the shopkeeper asked me directly as I placed my goods on the counter. "You're up there sorting her stuff, aren't you?"

"Yes, I am sorting her stuff for the estate. I'm Andy North. Do you really think that man will turn up at her house?" I hoped my acting was good enough to convince them. "What? Like a zombie?"

"That's a good one." The second woman thumped the counter with her fist and roared a deep, lusty laugh. "A zombie! Ha, with Gunna, you wouldn't notice any difference. He looks like a zombie in his Sunday best."

The shopkeeper joined in with the laughter while I tried to look incredulous, even though a picture of Zombie Gunna floated in my imagination. They were right.

"No," the shopkeeper exclaimed as she tallied up my purchases, "but he lives up that way in a caravan, so if he isn't floating in the lake, stands to reason you might see him up there."

"Oh, that old caravan down by the lake?" I kept up my pretence of ignorance. "I can just see that out Maggie's windows. The police came and checked it, so I assume he isn't there."

As they continued to discuss whether or not Gunna would reappear, I paid for my groceries and left, promising I would let them know if I saw anything strange and knowing I had already broken that promise. I did my best to stick to the speed limit driving back to Maggie's house.

Chapter 10

Back at the house, I couldn't settle and found myself pacing aimlessly through the rooms, picking up objects and putting them down without consciously noticing I was doing it, checking my watch every few minutes and racing to the window every time I convinced myself I heard a vehicle coming up the gravel road. I avoided looking over at the woolshed, riddled with a ridiculous paranoia that somehow, from the police station miles away, Carlton would see me looking at the shed and all our plans would fall through. When the paranoia got so intense that I began talking to myself out loud, I forced myself to go outside where I could walk around the whole house and glance over at the woolshed without it looking obvious to the omniscient eyes of my imaginary watcher.

Walking didn't help. I was hearing noises all around me and I jumped at every one of them. From the lake the mournful cry of a bird made me shiver, then the garage door rattled in the light breeze and froze me to the spot before common sense made me keep walking to where I could see the woolshed looking completely normal. Shaking my head at my own gullibility, I went back inside and was just about to turn on the electric jug to make coffee when I really did hear a car approaching. Bruno was smiling when he burst through the door.

"The shit is about to hit the fan," he grinned.

"Where's Gunna?"

"Driving with the plain clothes cop to show him where to

come."

"Isn't he worried people will see him?"

"Apparently, according to his logic, the locals would look at me as they know my car but, as it's a main road, they won't look twice at a car they don't recognise, so Gunna reckons nobody will notice him as long as they drive through the town without stopping. Anyway, they shouldn't be too far behind me. Gunna's going to show him the body bits in the woolshed then all hell is going to break loose. In fact, that sounds like them now. Let's go and join the circus."

We crossed the paddock to the woolshed where we met Gunna and Harris, the same detective I had met at the lake, who seemed surprised to meet me again. He shook my hand before Gunna led the way around the bottom of the shed and through the doors into the gloom of the pig pen. The stench was intense.

"Bloody hell!" Harris swore over the high-pitched squealing of the hungry pigs. "What the hell has he been doing in here?"

"Like we told your boss, illegal trading in wild meat and, just to top it off, killing a bloke and feeding his body to those guys," Gunna answered, motioning towards the pigs with a flick of his thumb.

Harris pulled a powerful torch from his pocket, turned it on and swept the light over the pile of swans.

"Bloody hell! So you reckon there's a man's body in there?"

"Yep." Bruno leant forwards and pointed to the odd bit of colour in the pile. "Right there. That's a bit of his jacket and his head's just a bit to the left. See, by the black wing."

"Don't touch it!" Harris leant forwards to grab Bruno's

arm. "Let's get back out into the fresh air and I'll call in the forensic guys." From behind their wire fence the pigs squealed. "And we'll need a vet to deal with those two."

"I'm a vet," Bruno reminded him. "There's an old guy up the road who's an expert on pigs. In fact, Gunna thinks these two have been stolen from his place. I'm sure he will take them, even if they're not his. I'll just have to go up there and borrow his trailer."

Harris was already heading back outside, sucking the fresh air into his lungs.

"Oh, hell that's just nasty in there. Right, you go get whatever you need to remove those pigs and I'll phone my team. They'll need to take photos of the pigs in situ but then we'll need them gone asap so we can set up some decent lighting in there and start working through that pile. Bloody hell, I don't think I've ever seen anything like that before."

There wasn't much Gunna or I could do, so we stood to one side while Harris spoke to someone on his phone and Bruno sprinted back across the paddock then drove away in the direction of van Rooy's farm.

"They're taking bets down at the pub on what day you will float up in the lake," I told Gunna. "And I've been warned that you might turn up at Maggie's house – oh that's right, you did."

Gunna chuckled. "Like a bad penny, I'm bound to turn up somewhere. Maybe tonight. I might just turn up at the pub for a beer. That would cause a bit of a ruction."

"Right," Harris turned to us, "The team is on its way and I've told them to keep radio silence so Carlton doesn't get wind of what's going on. I've also spoken to his immediate superior who's going to keep Carlton occupied so he won't have a chance to get up here before the team has done its work. So now we wait for them to get here. I don't suppose there's any chance of a cup of coffee while we wait?"

"Not a problem," I replied. "I'll go get us some. How do you like it?"

"Milk and two, thanks."

"Me, too," Gunna added.

I left the men talking, grateful for something to do as my paranoia was returning. I still felt as if I was being watched, even though I knew Carlton was nowhere near. It didn't take long to make three mugs of coffee, but climbing back through the fence without spilling them was too hard, so I took the long way, up Maggie's drive and along the road. From that angle the woolshed looked less dilapidated than it actually was. Carlton had obviously gone to some lengths to maintain the front so nothing that happened inside was visible to anyone driving past. I rejoined the two men who muttered their thanks as they took the warm mugs.

"The biggest problem," Harris said between sips, "is going to be pinning Carlton to this and making it stick. Unless we find good evidence, he can admit to owning the building but claim he never went near it so had no idea what it was being used for. This is going to get very tricky."

"Nah, I've got evidence," Gunna replied. "Photos, videos too, of him and Nettles. And I've got a log book – times, dates, everything you need."

"Good. That's really good. Now all we need is my team to arrive. Come on guys!"

As it was, Bruno arrived first, towing an enclosed tandem trailer and accompanied by a bent, grizzled old man who seemed much too small for the bushy, grey beard that covered all of his face except his rheumy blue eyes and fell almost to his waist. Bruno helped him down from the Land Rover's cab, introducing him as Hank van Rooy before leading him through the door into the smelly depths of the woolshed. After a few minutes they returned and van Rooy nodded.

"Yep, that's Helga and Hortense. I thought they'd wandered off up the back somewhere. Didn't realise some bugger'd stolen them. Soon as you like, I'll load 'em up and get 'em out of your hair."

"I guess you saw the pile of carcasses in there?" Harris asked. "Would those pigs really eat all of that? Could you really get rid of a body that way?"

"Yep. Yep, indeed you could. Pigs'll pretty much eat anything, although I'm not so sure about the feathers. They ain't fussy, 'specially if you keep 'em hungry and that's all they're gettin' fed. Not good for 'em though. I'll have to keep an eye on 'em for a while and get some decent feed into 'em. Poor old girls."

I was still struggling to think of the giant, shrieking monsters as poor old girls when two cars and a van pulled in through the gate. The forensic team had arrived. Bruno herded Hank to where Gunna and I were standing out of the way and we all watched, fascinated as the team swung into action and amused each time one of them rushed back out of the woolshed to vomit into the grass. Floodlights and a power generator were carried in, followed by a photographer, but we were kept firmly on the outside for over an hour before Harris gave Bruno the all-clear to remove the pigs. I hung back, preparing to hide as I expected the pigs to charge out and attack us, but instead, to everyone's amazement, Bruno cut the padlock to open the pen and Hank stepped forwards, called the pigs' names softly, and patted them on their wiry snouts. The two hulking beasts grunted, snuffled at his hand and peacefully followed him through the door and up the ramp onto the trailer.

"Well, I'll be buggered," Harris exclaimed. "Here was I, thinking we'd have to shoot them with a tranquiliser gun. This day just gets weirder by the minute. Mr van Rooy, Bruno," he ran to the trailer, "can you please keep those two in quarantine for a few days? We're going to need to collect their droppings to run forensic tests on."

"You want their poo as evidence?" Hank laughed.

"Yes, we do. We need proof of what they've been eating."

"Then you're welcome to all you can pick up. It's all yours."

"Thanks," Harris rounded on two constables standing near the door. "That will be a lovely job for whichever one of you pisses me off most this week." The constables avoided eye contact.

As Bruno helped Hank into the Land Rover, I asked Harris if Gunna and I could wait back at the house. Gunna declined the offer, preferring to stay and watch, but I had no desire to see the carcasses as they were brought out of the shed so I was relieved when Harris agreed I could leave.

Back at the house, I rinsed out the coffee mugs and poured myself another cup, then forced my reluctant brain into work mode. A check of my inventory list showed I had nearly finished itemising all the contents of the house, and the shed full of taxidermied birds and strange tools, so that left only the garage to deal with. With a bit of luck, the birds and tools would all belong to Gunna and I wouldn't have to touch any of them. Gunna would have to move them, but where he would move them to? The caravan wasn't big enough. Would he have to move the caravan too? It was on Maggie's land and if the house was sold, the new owners might not want a weird old hippy camping on their lakefront. I wished they had got around to getting married. Gunna's future looked bleak.

Fortified by coffee, biscuits and determination, I shut off thoughts of what was happening in the woolshed and concentrated on Maggie's extensive wardrobe, leaving the vintage collectible clothes on their colour-co-ordinated hangers and shelves, but throwing the everyday pieces, such as her flannelette nightgowns and underwear, into black rubbish bags to be dumped. I was engrossed in a shelf of felt hats when Bruno found me to tell me he had delivered Hank and the pigs and was heading back to his veterinary practice in Mosgiel.

"Amy has left me six messages, each one grumpier than the last," he said, "so I'd better show my face."

Amy, I had forgotten about Amy. I'd be grumpy too if my boyfriend hadn't been home all night.

"Give Jackson a pat for me," was all the response I could force myself to give.

"Will do. I'll be back later. I'll bring food."

Then he was gone. I felt flat, empty. Damn Amy. As he drove away I couldn't concentrate and found myself walking to the lounge without any real purpose. I stepped out onto the deck to get a better look at the police team still busy at the woolshed but, much as I was curious to know what was happening, I knew I wouldn't be told anything, so going over there was pointless. Gunna would fill me in when he returned. Back to work.

Gunna found me an hour later, hugging and stroking a fur coat.

"It's so soft," I offered as an excuse for my odd behaviour. "Is it mink?"

"No, just good old bunny rabbit," Gunna replied. "Maggie shot them."

"You're kidding?"

"Nope, told you she was a good shot. I know fur's not fashionable anymore but Maggie looked on it as recycling. They're a pest around here and have to be culled, so she found a good use for them. Made a great rabbit stew too."

"And this one?" I pulled a jacket from the wardrobe.

"Possum. Trapped by me."

"Oh." I wasn't sure if the coats still held the appeal they did before Gunna told me where they came from. I changed the subject. "How's it going over at the woolshed?"

"They're packing up for the day but I think they'll be back tomorrow. They've bagged up all the dead swans and found several bits of whoever that poor bastard is, but from what Harris is muttering, identifying him is going to be a hard job. There's not a lot left but, hopefully, my photos will help. I'd love to be a fly on the wall at the police station though."

"Why?"

"Because Harris has taken a couple of constables with him and he's off to arrest Carlton."

"Arrest him? Did they find enough evidence to do that?"

"Not sure, maybe arrest is the wrong word. Hold him for questioning, that's what Harris said."

"I wonder if he will plead ignorance or drop Nettles right in it?"

"Both, I reckon," Gunna said. "He'll weasel out of it any way he can. Still, I've given Harris my camera with some pretty incriminating photos on it and I'm here to sort some more of my files so I can give them to him tomorrow."

Gunna left me re-hanging, counting and noting the fur coats so when Bruno finally arrived back carrying a parcel of fish and chips, I had a smug feeling of accomplishment, which didn't last long.

"Harris rang me," Bruno threw his Swanndri onto a chair and faced me. "Carlton has done a bunk."

"What?"

"Harris expected him to be at the police station but he never turned up. His police car is there but his own car has gone."

"Oh, shit."

"Yeah, Harris is pretty pissed off. I wouldn't want to be the person who slipped Carlton the warning, if anybody did. Harris is wondering if he had some sort of alarm system attached to the gate. I offered to go and have a look for one but he's warning us to stay well away. If Carlton's spooked, he might be dangerous."

"Great. Are we safe here tonight?"

"We should be but let's draw the curtains and lock all the doors, just in case."

"That fills me with confidence – not."

"Let's not worry about it. There's a constable standing guard up at the woolshed, so if Carlton turns up there, he's going to get caught, but I'm still going to listen out for any cars going up the road. In the mean time, where's Gunna? These fish and chips'll be cold if we don't eat them soon."

Sitting cross-legged on the floor in front of a stoked-up,

roaring fire, eating fish and chips out of their newspaper wrapping, seemed a world away from the horrors of the woolshed. As I didn't want to be reminded of the pile of carcasses while I was eating, I banned any talk of it. Instead, our dinner held the same surreal quality of domesticity I had felt before. It wasn't somebody else's house that I was staying in, it was my house, my friends (or did they feel more like family?) and my warm, comforting fire. All I needed was my dog, which made me feel sad as I knew in my heart I needed to give Jackson to Gunna, who obviously loved him dearly and who had lost enough when Maggie died.

I was laughing at Gunna's stories of Bruno as a schoolboy when I heard a car stop outside and a car door slam shut. We all froze as footsteps pounded up the steps. As a fist knocked on the door, Gunna slipped away through the bookcase into the secret room. I called out "Who is it?" as Bruno positioned himself out of sight behind the door.

"Ian Carlton," the response came. "I've brought you the printed version of your statement for your insurance."

"Okay, just a minute." I stalled for time, shrugging and mouthing a "what do I do?" message to Bruno. He looked unsure so I decided to be brave, stepped forwards and opened the door. To the side I could see Bruno texting furiously, presumably to Harris.

"Hi," I greeted Carlton as cheerfully as I could fake. "That's very kind of you. You didn't need to come all this way, but I do appreciate it." I took the piece of paper he offered, hoping he would leave, but he stood firm.

"Have you noticed anyone up at my shed today?" he asked.

"No, no," I lied. "I haven't looked out the windows much,

to be honest. I've been trying to get my job finished here so I can go home, so I've spent all day stuck in Maggie's giant walk-in wardrobe, listing her vintage clothes. Her wardrobe's massive," I prattled on, "there's one whole rack just of fur coats. It was getting dark by the time I'd finished, so, no, I haven't had time to notice anything else. Why? Has something happened? Have they found Gunna?"

"I don't know," Carlton shifted on his feet, turning to look over his shoulder. "That's McTavish's rover isn't it? What's he doing here this late? Are you two at it?"

"At what? Oh, I get what you're implying. Actually," I paused, breathing deeply as rising anger flushed the last vestiges of fear away, "I was going to say that he brought me news of Jackson but now I'm going to tell you that, if we were 'at it', even if we were bonking like rabbits, it's no bloody business of yours. So thanks for bringing the statement, sorry, no I haven't spotted Gunna in your woolshed and good night."

I stepped back, shut the door quickly and turned the key to lock it. Beside me Bruno smothered a laugh, clutching his hand to his mouth until we heard the car door slam and the engine start, then he let the laughter splutter out in shaking gasps.

"Oh my god, you were brilliant. I wish I could have seen his face. I didn't know we were bonking like rabbits."

"In your dreams," I swatted him on the arm. I wondered if it was in his dreams, it had certainly been in mine. "Be serious. Did you get hold of Harris?"

"Yep. He's sending a car and he's radioed the constable who's guarding the woolshed."

"So what do we do?"

"Hmm, I was going to say we do nothing but I've got a better idea. Back in a tick."

Bruno took his keys from the pocket of his Swanndri and left, returning a few minutes later carrying a futuristic-looking rifle and a small bag.

"Dart gun," he said before I could ask. "I had it on stand-by for the pigs and now I'm wondering if it might be just the job for stopping Carlton. At least it would hold him until Harris gets here."

"That's too dangerous," I argued. "He'll see you coming. What if he thinks it's a real rifle and shoots you first?"

"He won't see me, trust me." Bruno pulled on his Swanndri and covered his blond-streaked hair with a dark green beanie. "I'm betting he's too busy checking out what's missing inside the shed to bother looking across the paddock. Don't worry, I'll be careful."

I wasn't convinced but he wasn't going to be dissuaded so I bit back my protests and walked out into the darkness with him, holding the dart gun while he climbed the fence. I was standing in the lee of the stairs, watching him walk away across the paddock into the darkness, when a hand covered my mouth and pulled me backwards. Carlton was still here? I tried to scream but the hand over my mouth was strong, then a sharp object stuck into my ribs and a familiar voice warned me to be quiet.

"Bonking like rabbits. I knew you were. You slut." The hand forced my head back while another grabbed my hair and yanked, pulling my body backwards towards the garage. "You thought I'd given up and gone away, but I don't walk away from things I own and I own you. Mother is not happy with your behaviour. Neither am I."

Sir kicked the garage door open, pulled me inside then spun e around so my back was bent over the bonnet of spur's beautiful car. He changed his grip so his left hand M'ow holding my mouth shut, freeing his right hand to t my clothing. I struggled, flailing my arms at his back, he pushed me harder into the car's bonnet, giving me no tion to move or fight. The fastener on my jeans popped pen. As his hand slid down into my knickers, my muscles tensed. I squirmed under him, trying to breathe, to scream, to get away. I screamed for Bruno in my head but the only sound I could make was muffled by Simon's grip. How could I get attention? Underneath me the metal of the car bonnet flexed with Simon's weight added to mine. His fingernails scratched my hip as he tried to remove my jeans. I squirmed more, struggling to move my legs. If I could get them up onto the bumper, could I get enough traction to push him off? How could I get Bruno's attention? Was he too far away now to hear me? What could I use to make enough noise? With all my strength I flung my arms sideways, drumming my fists onto the car's metal, banging out the old Morse code for SOS that my father had taught me when I was a child playing spy games.

Simon pulled his hand out of my jeans long enough to slap my face hard.

"From the look of him, you've decided you like it rough, well rough you're going to get. Go on, struggle a bit harder, you're turning me on."

"And I'm turning you off." With a surprised grunt, Simon fell sideways as Gunna's concerned face swam into focus.

"Are you all right, lass? Did he hurt you? Who the hell is he?"

I let Gunna help me to my feet, studied 〷on's unconscious form, noting the heavy piece of wo in Gunna's hand before pulling back my foot and deliv Simon a hefty kick to his ribs.

"This, Gunna, is my despicable, controlling, narcissist ex." I punctuated my description with a solid kick with every word. "I thought I had escaped from him when I flew down here but the bastard followed me, then I thought he had given up when he ran into Bruno who told him where to go and how to get there. I thought he had run back to his ghastly mother in Wellington. Seems I was mistaken." I kicked him again.

"Okay, okay," Gunna pulled me gently out of kicking distance. "Well, what are we going to do with him now?"

"I could give him an overdose of this," Bruno's voice spoke from the door. "Or I could get my vet bag and cut his nuts off. Without an anaesthetic."

Before he could put down the dart gun, I had flown across the garage and thrown myself into Bruno's arms, sobbing into his chest as the adrenalin leaked away. Gunna held his hand out to take the rifle and Bruno wrapped me in a hug, planting tiny kisses on the top of my head as I snuggled into the warmth of his chest. When the sobs died to a sniffle, Gunna got our attention with a discreet cough.

"Enough canoodling, you two. I need some help to sort out this piece of shit."

Reluctantly, I lifted my hands to Bruno's chest and stepped back from his arms. After one more kiss and a smile, he moved to help Gunna who had found some cable ties and was securing Simon's wrists and ankles. As he worked, Simon started to wake up, but even fully conscious and struggling, he was no match for Bruno who dragged him to the wall where he shackled him to a convenient metal hook.

"Can I cut his nuts off now?" Bruno asked with a deliciously evil grin.

Simon struggled against his bindings, sobbing "No, no, no," as he scrabbled as far away from Bruno as he could manage.

"No, not yet," I said, stepping forwards to stand over my cowering ex. "Maybe later. First, though, you'd better pretend he's an animal we care about and check his head. We don't want Gunna blamed for helping me."

Bruno's response was an angry glare but he did as I asked, although with less care and consideration than he would have used on even the worst-tempered animal patient.

"He'll live," he declared. "Pity. What do you want to do with him?"

"Let's leave him here for now. I'm sure Detective Harris is driving this way at speed, as we speak, and I'm sure he'll be only too happy to take this bastard back with him, throw him in a comfy cell and charge him with attempted rape. Mummy will be so proud."

Bruno put his arm around my shoulder and we walked away, leaving Simon alternatively whimpering and yelling abuse as he struggled against the sturdy metal hook securing him to the wall. With Gunna following, carrying the dart gun, we stepped out into a bright light that lit the view across the paddock.

"Holy shit," Bruno exclaimed. "The woolshed's on fire! Andy, ring triple 1. Gunna, get hold of Harris. I'm going up there."

"No!" I grabbed his arm. "Stay here. There's nothing we

can do. Carlton could still be there. He's dangerous."

"The constable! The guy Harris left there. I've got to make sure he's safe."

Gunna was already on his phone as Bruno leapt over the fence and ran. I pulled mine out and dialled, watching Bruno run towards the flames as I gave details to the emergency operator.

"Harris isn't far away," Gunna said as I hung up. He had his phone in camera mode and was clicking furiously, capturing the flames leaping in orange, red and yellow fingers upward into the black sky. Framed against the light, Bruno was a silhouette, a black shape getting smaller as he raced towards the inferno.

"No!" I cried as I saw him dart towards the small door and enter the burning building. Then I was running too, scaling the fence and pounding over the rough ground. Behind me I heard Gunna call, faint against the roar of the flames. I ran on.

The heat hurt my throat and lungs as I breathed it in. My eyes stung but I kept running towards the black gap of the doorway. I yelled Bruno's name, hoping I would see him smiling and safe. Then I did. I reached the door, staying in the centre of the gap, afraid of the glowing wood that crackled around me. Inside, past where the swans had been piled, deep in the pig pen, I saw a movement. I called out and the hunched figure lifted its head.

"Stay back, I've got him," Bruno shouted.

He hunkered down again and I realised he was dragging something, someone. I took a deep breath, drawing up the courage to step through the doorway to help, when the air seemed to change. The flames grew brighter, louder, as the timbers above Bruno shattered, tumbling around him in a burning waterfall of embers, covering him as he fell to the ground.

"Bruno! Bruno!" I leapt forwards, thrusting through the falling debris, ignoring the heat, choking on the smoke as I shoved blackened pieces of wood out of my way. The pig pen was their saviour; the sturdy wire gates had created a barrier against the falling roof. Bruno was huddled against them, protecting the unconscious police constable with his body. I sank to my knees beside them, wanting to hold Bruno tight but knowing there was no time to waste.

"Come on," I urged, "we need to go."

Dazed, Bruno stared at me, not comprehending, then shook himself like a wet dog and smiled, his teeth abnormally white against his soot-blackened face. He wrapped his arms under the shoulders of the young constable and motioned for me to grab his feet.

"Let's do this."

Together, we lifted the injured man and carried him out as the building collapsed around us.

Chapter 11

Outside, safe from the flames, we lowered the constable gently to the ground and collapsed beside him, arms wrapped around each other as we gasped for breath. I pulled Bruno tight, resting my head against his shoulder, feeling his breath ruffling my hair. His hands moved to cup my chin towards his face, towards the kiss that obliterated the fire around us.

Then we were surrounded by men in fluorescent yellow coats who rushed to our aid, separating us, covering our mouths with oxygen masks and wrapping us in warm blankets. As my mind cleared I realised my hands ached. I held them out in front of me, palms up and saw the look of concern deepen on the face of the firefighter who had given me the mask. He raised an arm for attention then led me towards the fire engines where he handed me over to another yellow coat who was carrying a first aid kit.

"We need to get your hands under cold water," he said.

"I'll take her." Gunna appeared by my side. "There's a trough over by the fence. Come on, I'll take you over there."

"All right," the firefighter agreed. "Get cold water running and keep under it for at least ten minutes. The ambulance should be arriving shortly and as soon as they've dealt with the policeman, I'll send them over to check on you. You'll probably have to go to hospital to get those burns seen to."

I mumbled agreement and let Gunna lead me across the paddock to an ancient concrete water trough. It was empty, the bottom full of leaves and a green slime with an offensive smell, but Gunna wasn't put off. He twisted the trough's rusted tap, suggesting we stood back while the tap belched orange water in air-bubble driven bursts. When it slowed to a steady, clear stream, I thrust my hands into it, letting the icy cold relieve the sting of the reddening burns.

From my position, precariously perched on the edge of the trough, bent into the running water, I watched firemen playing their hoses over the woolshed, fighting a losing battle with the flames that thrived on the aged, dry wood. The cold from my concrete seat seeped through my body, making me shiver. Ten minutes under the icy water seemed like forever. I wanted to leave, to stand up straight from the uncomfortable position I was sitting in, to find Bruno. Had that kiss really happened? Why did it happen? What has happening between us? I was about to walk away when a medic found me, declared my burns superficial, applied two huge dressings held on by light bandages and advised me to see my doctor in the morning. I nodded agreement, lacking the energy to explain that I didn't have a doctor locally. Would a vet do?

The heat of the flames drew me back to the burning woolshed, now reduced to a giant bonfire of fallen wood, parts of it damp and steaming as the firefighters gained control. From the front of the shed Gunna waved, beckoning me to join him and Harris.

"They reckon they've found Carlton's body," Gunna said with grim smile. "In there."

"There's some barbed wire wrapped around his leg," Harris took up the story. "We're guessing he started the fire in the middle of the shed, then tripped over the wire when he was trying to get out. Hoist by his own petard, as my dad used to say."

"Why did he start the fire? If you guys had already been here, what was the point?"

"To get rid of the evidence. I'm guessing he didn't realise how much the forensic team have already retrieved. Maybe he thought he could bluff his way out of trouble if the shed and everything in it was gone."

"And in his panic, he's burnt himself to death. That's sad. Even if he was doing something stupid, according to Gunna he didn't kill that poor guy, Nettles did. Carlton must have been a good cop once, surely?"

"Oh yeah," Harris agreed. "He was a very good cop. Just not so good a person. A bit too reliant on keeping in good with his friends and, unfortunately, not choosing good people to be friends with."

"What about the other policeman? Is he going to be all right?" I asked.

"Yeah, we hope so. He's had a decent knock to his head but he was coming round as the ambulance was loading him up to take him off to hospital. I'll go in when I'm finished here and check on him. Poor bugger, it's his first year on the job. Let's hope it doesn't put him off."

"Where's Bruno?"

Harris waved his torch towards a police car. "Giving a statement."

"Oh, do I need to do that too?"

"No, we'll get yours tomorrow. McTavish will be finished soon and you three will be able to get back into the warm. I'm looking forward to wrapping this up and getting home, myself."

I was about to agree when I remembered Simon.

"Simon!" I exclaimed, getting me perplexed looks from both men. "The ex." Gunna nodded, Harris still looked confused. "Detective Harris, can you come with me please? We have someone else we need you to take care of."

Bruno joined us while I was explaining my relationship with Simon and how my arrival for work was also my escape from his abuse. When I got to Simon's assault on me and his attempted rape, Harris swore, ordered us to follow him and led us across the paddock at a fast jog. We caught up with him as he squeezed himself between the wires of the fence.

"He's in here," Gunna said, hauling back the heavy garage door.

But he wasn't.

Where Simon had been trussed securely, we thought, to a firmly attached piece of metal, the light from Harris's torch framed just a gaping hole in the wall and a heap of splintered wood on the floor. A pair of wire cutters and a pile of severed cable ties lay on the adjacent work bench.

"Damn and blast it!" Gunna swore. "I knew that wood was getting soft. I was gunna replace it."

"He can't have gone far," Harris said, sweeping the beam of the torch around as if he expected to find him hiding under the car.

"Just back to Wellington," I said. "He must have had a car parked up somewhere. My guess is, he's running back to mummy as fast as he can."

"Right. Let's go back up to the woolshed so I can use my car's radio. I'll send someone to check out Momona airport and we'll catch him if he tries to get on a plane. You can give me his details as we walk."

Harris and I automatically headed towards the fence but

Gunna called our attention to the ground in the opposite direction.

"Look! Swing the light over here. He went this way. Towards the lake."

The flattened grass didn't look much different to me but Harris nodded in agreement.

"Good spotting, but there's no point following him in the dark. If he hasn't made his way to the road and hitched a lift, he won't get far, and if he has hitched a lift we'll pick him up when he tries to fly back to Wellington. Either way, us floundering about in the dark isn't going to help. Ms North, you need to go inside and get yourself warm, you're shivering. I'm going to go back up to my car so I can call this in and organise some of those eager young constables to round up this guy as soon as it gets light."

I was shivering, with cold but also with a new-found fear. Simon was still out there, hunting me.

"What if Gunna's wrong and Simon's already inside the house, waiting for me to return?" I asked. "I'm not sure I want to go back inside."

But Gunna was right. The three men searched the house, opening wardrobes and even pulling back the bookcase entry to the secret rooms, which had Harris gasping in wonder. With all the lights turned on and no places left unsearched, I began to relax, the tension that had kept me upright giving way to tiredness as the fear faded away. Wrapped cocoon-like in a blanket, I curled up on the couch, vaguely aware of Harris leaving and Bruno stoking the fire with more wood before I fell asleep.

I was woken by a mumble of voices and the smell of bacon cooking. Bruno, looking fresh from a shower, his muscles highlighted by a clinging white t-shirt, was frying eggs. He looked across at me, flicking the habitually untidy lock of hair from his eyes, and I was suddenly hungry. Okay, for more than just breakfast but with the room full of police, breakfast was the only thing on the menu. Shame. With an embarrassed smile to the blue uniforms camped around the dining table, I unthreaded myself from the blanket and scuttled to the bedroom in search of clean clothes. I wanted a shower but I couldn't work out how to do that without getting the bandages on my hands wet, so I settled for cleaning my teeth and trying to drag a brush through my hair. There were times when I was glad I hadn't listened to Simon's repeated demands to grow it long.

In clean clothes, including another of Maggie's huge and bizarrely-coloured knitted jerseys that hung down almost to my knees, I followed the enticing smell of food back to the kitchen, accepting a plate from Bruno and squeezing into a space at the table between Harris and Gunna. In stark contrast to Bruno's refreshed look, Harris and Gunna were bleary-eyed and still soot-covered from the woolshed fire. Behind me, daylight was beginning to seep around the edge of the curtains.

"Have you caught him yet?" I asked Harris.

"No, but we know where he is." Harris rubbed the greying stubble of his unshaven chin. "Gunna, here, has already been out for a reconnoitre and says he's holed up in the caravan, so we're making plans to go and collect him. As you can see, I've mustered up a few extra bodies so he won't get far if he tries to run."

I nodded around a large piece of bacon that I had stuffed in my mouth, unable to cut it into smaller pieces as trying to eat gracefully was making my hands ache. While I chewed, Harris explained his plans to the three uniformed officers on the other side of the table, moving coffee cups and the salt shaker around the table to illustrate his speech. He let us finish our meal then looked at his watch, checked the daylight through the window and called us into action.

"Let's get this bastard."

Gunna took the lead, moving at speed over the paddock towards the lake. The rest of us fumbled along behind him, trying not to trip on the myriad of rabbit holes that littered the ground. As we approached his ancient caravan, Gunna stopped, raising an arm to warn us to do the same.

"This is where we split up," he said. "Bruno, you and you," he pointed to one of the constables, "fan out over to the right. You other two go left. Detective, you and I will sneak right up to the caravan door."

"What about me?" I asked.

"Stay here." Harris and Gunna said in unison. I followed them.

It should have been easy but Simon must have heard us approaching, so we were all still too far away when he burst out of the caravan door. At first he was running directly towards Bruno and the constable but as soon as they broke cover and ran towards him, he changed direction, bolting towards the lake. We all followed but Gunna stopped us when the ground underneath us changed from solid to swamp.

"He's got nowhere to go now," Gunna said. "He's a city boy in city shoes, he's not going to get very far. No use us all getting wet. Bruno and I know our way around these waters. You guys don't and, with all due respect to your uniforms, I don't want to have to rescue you guys too. We'll sing out if we need help."

Ahead of us I could see Simon floundering through the reeds, his impeccable Italian suit coat flapping behind him as he stumbled. Bruno and Gunna laughed as they waded after him, impervious to the wet in their gumboots and thick, woollen Swanndri jackets.

"You may as well give up and come back," Harris yelled to the fleeing figure. "Don't make things any worse than they are."

I held my breath as Bruno and Gunna covered the ground fast, Gunna's knowledge of the dry paths giving them a huge advantage over Simon who was thigh deep as he thrashed through the reeds. Suddenly Simon seemed to rise up as he found a patch of dry land. With a backwards glance at us, he ran forwards. In front of him I saw the reeds shake. Simon screamed.

He turned back, his face contorted in horror as a figure launched out of the reeds towards him. With his head low and his huge wings spread wide in anger, Herman the swan ran at Simon, honking his displeasure. Simon, terrified, tried to run but stumbled into the swamp, aided by Herman who flew onto his back, pushing him down into the water, his wings slapping as he drove his beak into Simon's prostrate body.

From the safety of the lake's edge we waited, our breaths held in anticipation, but Simon didn't get up. Gunna motioned Bruno to stay then calmly approached the angry swan who responded to Gunna's quiet voice and retreated to its nest. Gunna pulled Simon from the water and checked his pulse, then looked up at us and shook his head. Why didn't I feel sad?

In fact, I felt no emotion at all as I watched Gunna and Bruno carry Simon's body to dry land. I chose not to look at him, his usually neat hair plastered to his face, his suit sodden, not because it grieved me to see him, but because I realised that I didn't care at all. If I felt anything, it was a sense of relief that, finally, that era of my life was over. There was nothing to tie me to Wellington now. I walked away, leaving him to the police. Bruno joined me, wrapping his arm tight around my shoulders as I left the past behind me.

Inside the comforting warmth of the house, Bruno drew me into his arms, his soft kiss becoming deeper and more passionate as I responded. Until I stopped and pushed him away.

"We can't do this," I sighed. "What about Amy?"

"Who? What?" Bruno shook his head in confusion.

"Amy. Your girlfriend. Remember her? The one who sends you texts asking where you are and when you're coming home. That Amy."

"Oh, no, no, Amy's..." Bruno pulled his phone out of his pocket, hit an icon then rapidly typed some letters. "Here, I'll show you."

When he turned the screen towards me I saw a photo of six people, all dressed in white lab coats, posed outside the veterinary clinic. Bruno scrolled the screen and another photo filled it. A cheerful, round face smiled at the camera, laughing green eyes offset by a mass of unruly red curls.

"This is Amy," Bruno smiled. "She's married to a mechanic, has three children and does dog agility with the ugliest dog you've ever seen. She's also the best vet nurse in the universe. Oh, and on Fridays she brings us cupcakes. Yes, she is always sending me grumpy texts, but that's because I drive her nuts, never being where I am supposed to be. You'll love Amy, we all do. Now, any other objections or can we try that kiss again?"

"Only one objection," I answered, my heart dropping. "I have to go back to Wellington."

"Why? Can't you stay here? Do you really have to go back?" Before I could answer, he pulled me towards him and our kiss drowned out my objections.

This time we were interrupted by Gunna who burst through the door, rubbing his hands in glee, a wide smile accentuating the gaps in his teeth.

"Oops, sorry," he said, shrugging an apology when he realised what he had interrupted. "Harris said to tell you he's sending someone to get your statements, Andy, one for the woolshed fire and one about Simon."

I laughed at Gunna's obvious embarrassment, gave Bruno a quick peck on his cheek and moved to look out the window, Simon's body was lying on the ground, two policemen standing beside it.

"What are they doing with him" I asked.

"Waiting for an ambulance to take him away."

"What about Carlton?"

"Yeah, him too. They haven't moved him yet. The firemen are still dampening the shed down. It's still too hot. It's gunna be a long day."

Which it was. I gave my statements to the policewoman who had been part of the hunt for Simon, then let Bruno change the dressings on my hands for sterile dressings and clean bandages from his vet's bag before he drove back to Mosgiel to attend to his work. An ambulance pulled into the drive and I watched out of the window while two medics zipped Simon into a black body bag, loaded him onto a gurney and took him away. Harris and his team came and went, using our kitchen as a temporary office, drinking our coffee and eating delicious scones that Gunna whipped up from Maggie's hand-written recipe book.

I couldn't settle. Bruno's question, why did I have to go back to Wellington, rattled around in my brain, disturbing my concentration, unsettling my life. What did I have to go back to? A tiny apartment and a job I was sick of. What would I do if I didn't go back? I couldn't stay in this house that I had already started to think of as home. It wasn't mine. Sadly, it wasn't even Gunna's, even though it should have been. I flopped despondently onto the couch and pulled Maggie's file towards me.

"Gunna," I got his attention and he sat down beside me. "I'm almost finished with Maggie's stuff but I've got a problem. Technically, I should just sell everything but I think you need to go through this house first. There must be a few of Maggie's things that you'd like to keep, so I'd like you to take anything you want and I will take them off the official chattels list. It's not going to make much difference to the value; once the property is sold the wildlife trust is still going to inherit quite a substantial amount of money."

"The wildlife trust?" Gunna's head shot up. "What wildlife trust?"

"The one she left everything too," I explained. I pulled a piece of paper out of the file and read out the name. "The Herman Swan Wildlife Trust. Didn't you know that?"

"Herman Swan. Well, I'll be buggered. Maggie, the old duck, she did it. She left it all to Herman Swan. I don't believe it. It's all mine. She left it to me after all." Gunna leant back into the couch, shaking his head in disbelief. I looked at him, confused. "Herman Swan, get it?" Gunna said. "It was a joke." He sat forwards, his voice serious. "It was Maggie's idea. She founded a trust, named it after that big, old swan who just did for your ex. She donated the money from her book to it, then used the money to fight for local wildlife. But there are only two directors, Maggie and myself, so..."

"This house and everything in it now belongs to the trust, and you are the sole director of the trust, so you can keep the house and live in it and it doesn't have to be sold," I finished for him.

"Well, bugger that!" Gunna said.

We were still sitting, hunched together, sorting through papers when Jackson hobbled through the door, tail wagging furiously. I made space on the couch and helped him up, careful not to touch his injured leg, then went to hug Bruno while Gunna cuddled the dog who snuggled into Gunna's lap. I pulled Bruno into the kitchen and explained about the trust and how Gunna was now the legal owner of the property.

"Which means I have no reason to stay here any longer."

"Which means you have every reason to stay here and nothing to go back to Wellington for," Bruno contradicted me.

"But I have no job here and nowhere to live," I argued.

"Of course you do," Gunna called from the couch. "The Herman Swan Wildlife Trust is a real thing. It gets real money. Maggie was the brains behind it. I can't run it by myself. It'll need a new director. Someone young, like you. Plus, this house is way too big for one old man. It's huge.

Plenty of room for us both. Anyway, Jackson needs you."

I looked at three sets of eyes; Bruno's sparkling with love, Gunna's and Jackson's doleful and pleading. I looked around the room, feeling again the comfortable sense of belonging that encompassed me whenever I was inside the house. I pulled my phone from my pocket and sent a text to my boss.

I quit.

I was too busy kissing Bruno to read her reply.

Other Books by J.L. O'Rourke

Power Ride
An Avi Livingstone Murder Mystery

Kester (Kit) Simmons, drummer with the rock band 'Charlotte Jane', was out of beat. He was stressed out, starving and he thought he was going crazy. Then, with less than two weeks to go before a national tour, Kit's precious drums and one of the band members are found slashed to pieces. The keyboard player, Avi Livingstone, is missing, Kit has no alibi and, to make matters worse, the police suspect him of dealing drugs.

Read an excerpt:
The weary-looking blond was not amused.

"Stop!" His shouted command cut through the sound pumping from the Marshall amplifiers, stopping his five fellow musicians in mid bar.

"Hold it!" The blond spun round to face the drummer.

"Kit, it's no bloody good, man. It's not bloody working. And it's not bloody good enough. What's with you, man? This is old hat! We've done it a million times, a dozen already today. You're always telling me you can do this number in your sleep; so sleep then, because today you sure as hell can't do it when you're awake!"

The man half-hidden behind the rack of shining black Tama drums moved both his sticks to his right hand, freeing his left to push a lock of long, sweat-dampened black hair back into place.

"I'm sorry," he said softly. "It's just... I'm a bit... um... I'm just not very together."

"We noticed."

"Look, can we take a break? I don't feel so good."

The blond shrugged and, as an answer, unstrapped his ageing Gibson guitar and propped it up onto a conveniently placed support stand.

"Why not? It certainly can't make this damned rehearsal go any worse."

Kester Simmons pushed the unruly lock of hair back into place again then unthreaded his long, lean body from behind his drums.

"I really am sorry, Danny," he sighed.

The blond replied with a savage glare.

"I don't want apologies, Kit, I want a drum beat. Damn it all, Kit, it just isn't good enough. We are hitting the road on tour in just over a week - ten days to be precise - and this rehearsal has been a complete bloody disaster!" Daniel Gordon was working himself into a mild frenzy.

Kester turned to walk away but Danny had wound himself up and continued his harangue.

"And another thing, Mr Simmons! If your 'not feeling too good' means what it usually does, you'd better get your act together and you had better do it damned fast. It's a long tour and we're not babysitting you through it this time. You had better be on deck all the bloody way!" His voice dropped to a malicious hiss. "Don't you forget for one minute, Kit, that we are running real close to not making this tour at all, and it's all your fault."

Blood in the Wings
The First of Severn

Vampires and murder backstage in a Christchurch theatre. 16 year old Riley Lowe is working as a stage hand, backstage at her theatre company's annual show. Her classmate from school, Tasha, is also in the show as a dancer and, as usual, she is flirting with all the guys. In particular, she is trying to take the one Riley is attracted to. Severn is one of a group of professional theatre crew who are helping with the show but the closer she gets to him, the more Riley realises that there is something strange about the group who live and work in the dark. When Tasha is killed and Severn disappears, Riley learns their terrible secret. But can she solve the murder in time to save Severn?

Read an excerpt:

The rain came down red and Severn was gone.

The police asked me lots of questions, both at the theatre and, later, down at the police station but I couldn't tell them much more than that. No, that's not true. I could have told them heaps more, but I didn't. Anyway, I wasn't sure myself. No, don't tell anyone anything. Just answer their questions, get out of here, find Severn and hope the answers are wrong.

"Tell me again, Miss Lowe, take it slowly." The policeman, a detective inspector I think he said he was, kept tapping his pen against the table. It was driving me crazy. The policewoman sitting by the door smiled. That was driving me crazy too.

"What do you know about this Severn?"

I have to think about the answer. I know things about

Severn that nobody knows but I hardly know him at all. And I desperately want to keep on learning.

So, really slowly like the cop wants, I start from the beginning again.

"I met Severn two weeks ago when we packed in." It feels like forever.

"Packed in?" the cop inquires.

"Yeah, that's what I said. Pack-in. It's theatre-speak, Get used to it!" This guy was so dumb.

"All right, Miss Lowe," the cop snapped. "There's no need to get abusive. Let's just get on with it so we can all go home."

"Yeah, well don't butt in then!" Okay, it was well after midnight and I was tired and cranky, but he really was a jerk. "I told you, I met him at pack-in. That's when we set up the show in the theatre." I added the last bit slowly, just in case he was as stupid as he looked in his prissy black jacket and his ugly blue tie,

Chains of Blood
The Second of Severn

Riley Lowe is backstage at another show, but this time she is out of her depth, running equipment she doesn't understand and faced with all sorts of problems including a boy actor who is a spoilt little brat. When her personal vampires arrive to help, Riley thinks everything has suddenly got better, until the boy disappears. Will the vampire's special skills be enough to find the boy and how long will it be before Riley turns into a vampire herself?

Out for Blood
The Third of Severn

The body on New Brighton beach has made headline news, the Reverend and Aiden are keeping secrets from Severn, and Riley believes someone is following her. When a video of Aiden flying goes viral, religious panic puts the vampires' identify and secrets under threat. As they try to solve the mystery of the body, Riley and Severn discover connections with the past and take their human and vampire relationships to new levels, but can they find a solution to present events before the Guild is exposed?

Blood Exposed
The Fourth of Severn

Riley's best friend, Anita, has convinced Riley and Severn to provide the technicals for a medieval re-enactment and fantasy convention run by the grandparent's of Anita's unborn baby, but they won't be paid because one of the committee has stolen the society's funds. Riley's attempts to find out who took the money are complicated when one of the committee is killed during the jousting tournament. Can Riley work out the committee's secrets and how will the real vampires cope with two steampunk goths who want to be bitten? Is a fantasy convention the one place they can show their true colours?

About the Author

J. L. O'Rourke has worked as a journalist, sub-editor, free-lance writer and office administrator. When not writing, she enjoys being in a theatre, either onstage as a singer or backstage where she has been everything from floor crew to stage-manager. She lives on a tranquil olive grove in North Canterbury, New Zealand.

You can follow her on Facebook at
https://www.facebook.com/MillwheelPress
www.millwheelpress.co.nz